THE GALLOWS HOUSE

Lisa Gail Green

www.BOROUGHSPUBLISHINGGROUP.com

THE GALLOWS HOUSE
Copyright © 2019 Lisa Gail Green

ISBN: 978-1-951055-34-9

To Shona, who stays my best friend even
when she reads the scary stuff in my brain

ACKNOWLEDGMENTS

I'd like to thank my editor, Adi, and Michelle Klayman for seeing the promise in *The Gallows House*. I would also like to thank my writing partner and beta reader, Leslie Rose, for her early insights and encouragement, as well as the Santa Clarita RWA chapter. But most importantly, I'd like to thank the readers, without whom there would be no books—and that would truly be a horror story.

THE GALLOWS HOUSE

CHAPTER 1

Bailey moved alongside the crowd of students heading home, trying to tune out the shouts and laughter all around. Too much crazy filtered in, especially since last year. The year her life fell apart, and the year she became separate, yet still connected to the others. At first glance, anyone would see another teenage girl with a white backpack in jeans and a black tee beneath an oversized, worn plaid shirt. Totally average. Average height, average build, light brown hair pulled back in a ponytail, hazel eyes—if anyone bothered to get close enough to look—and black and white checked high-tops. What they wouldn't see was the invisible wall separating normal high school life from her.

She kept her focus straight ahead on the corner of Willow and Oak where she'd be able to breathe and force her shoulders to relax. Despite the California heat stubbornly clinging to October, less than a handful of students chose the shady path home down Willow. Bailey was one of them. In either direction, witches and gravestones had already begun to appear on houses and lawns, along with spiderwebs, skeletons, and zombies.

Actually, though far more decorations dotted the path down Oak, Willow had the market cornered on spooktacular. It wasn't the wide, winding street lined with mature trees and twisted branches. Or the lack of human activity. Both could be seen through a filter of quaint or eerie, depending on the mood of the onlooker. No. The sprawling estate in the center of the street, merely a few doors down from the turn to Bailey's home was the place people avoided even though they never noticed they were doing it.

Halloween in Shadow Springs was more of a month-long event than a single night, and if the thirty-first was the big feast it all led up to, then the Gallows House was the centerpiece. It had long held the esteemed title of Shadow Spring's most haunted house, for obvious reasons. The place was overgrown and abandoned. The last owners had moved out after only a month when Bailey was three, which left almost fifteen years of dereliction to add to the ambiance.

If anyone bothered to think about it—aside from Bailey, of course—they'd realize that creepier than disrepair and the innumerable visitations of teenage near-do-wells on the property, was that the house was still amazingly intact and unharmed. Sure, it could do with a good coat of paint and a gardener, but there were no broken windows. No termite-eaten boards. Only a house, alone, and sad-looking, with faded shutters hidden in a nest of weeds and vines. Even the wrap-around porch seemed sturdy enough to sit on the old swing and reminisce while watching the curtain-like branches of the giant weeping-willow on the front yard sway whether or not there was wind. Better to watch the actual branches move than the nonsensical shadows they cast on the house, the ones that seemed to move randomly no matter what time of day she looked.

Bailey slowed her steps as she approached the front. All the noise had died down to a nearly inaudible buzz the minute she set foot on the street, as though a curtain had fallen between her and the rest of Lincoln High's student and teacher population. The air was thicker here, and the shade of the tunnel of trees along the way made it chilly enough for Bailey to hug herself to keep warm. At least she assumed that's what it was. It could've been the house. She believed it held dark secrets, ones she was determined to uncover, but she had to be sensible about it. She couldn't merely ignore the scientific approach or rule out mundane-yet-unlikely reasons for a thirty-degree temperature drop at two-fifteen in the afternoon.

Pausing to stare up at the attic window that opened between the deep slope of the roof on either side, Bailey repeated her silent promise. *I will find out what happened to you, Caleb. I swear it.*

He wouldn't up and leave his family like that. He wouldn't leave *her*. She would have known if her brother had been depressed. She would've noticed something, and she would have stopped him.

A shadow in the attic window caught Bailey's attention and she narrowed her eyes, straining to see. But nothing happened. She was about to turn back toward home, when a light came on in the first floor and she about jumped out of her skin. *Holy shit.* She splayed a hand over her racing heart. No, there was definitely a reasonable explanation. Someone had started the electricity up again—obviously. But what did that mean?

Bailey searched for witnesses before setting foot on the cobbled path headed toward the double front doors. When she was close enough, she veered to the left and navigated a clump of bushes so she could see the side of the house. The garage door was open and a red pickup was inside, filled with everything from dining room chairs to mirrors and lamps. And the inside door to the house was open like an invitation.

She'd been trying to get inside for almost a year, and now the door was *open*. But… that meant someone was in there. For real. A person who didn't know her, but knew she probably wasn't supposed to be there. And if her father found out she'd been in the Gallows House, well, nothing good would come of it. Not after Caleb.

Before she could make up her mind, someone stepped out of the doorway and into the garage. When he made eye contact with her, he looked as shocked as she felt. A boy her age, only much taller, stood gaping, hands covered in workman's gloves, and dark hair tousled and peeking out from beneath a baseball cap. She realized, with some awkwardness, that they wore almost the same outfit. Black T-shirt and jeans, though his hung loose and showed signs of recent labor between the scuff marks on the knees and the dirt and dust layered on the front of his shirt, as though he'd wiped his hands there. The biggest brown eyes she'd ever seen widened as she cleared her throat and smiled before thrusting out a hand.

"Hi, I'm Bailey. And you are?"

"Hunter. I… I live here." His voice was low and raspy, like it hadn't been used much.

Bailey attempted to hide her shock and the question marks exploding in her brain.

"You just moved in? I didn't know anyone had bought the house."

"Um, yeah." Hunter pulled off his gloves and set them on the hood of the car, then stuffed his hands in his pockets. "Yeah, we started this morning. Are you a neighbor or something?"

"Yeah." *Something like that.* "I live a few doors down and around the corner, on Elm. I was on my way home from school and I saw the lights on, so I wanted to… to make sure no one had, you know, broken in."

"Nope. Just us. So, you go to Lincoln?" Hunter kicked at a stone inside the garage.

"Yeah. It's okay. I'm sure you'll do great there. Everyone's pretty chill."

Bailey stretched her lips into such a wide grin she wondered if it looked more like a grimace. It was the best she could do as far as forcing herself to be friendly. Maybe if she were nice enough he'd invite her inside. No one could be upset if she had a friend who lived there, right?

"Cool. Well, thanks for stopping by."

So much for an invitation to come in.

"Yeah, I guess I'll see you at school." Bailey gave a lame wave as she backtracked out of the garage.

She wanted to scream with frustration and had a sudden crazy urge to yank Hunter out of the house and tell him to run. But what was she supposed to say? *You have to go before it's too late. My brother killed himself, and I think it was this house that made him do it*? The only person she'd confided even a portion of that to was Charity, and they'd known each other since preschool. Hunter was a complete stranger, and not the friendliest one at that. Besides, lots of people goof around the Gallows House, searching for supposed spirits and don't end up dead. So there was no point in being an alarmist, especially when it wasn't likely to change this guy's mind about being there.

"Hey, little brother, who's this? You making friends already?"

Bailey turned back at the sound of another male voice. This guy wasn't quite as tall as Hunter, but less gangly and definitely more muscular. His dark hair matched his brother's but was gelled into a trendy style. And though his eyes sparkled with friendliness, they didn't match the size or depth of Hunter's.

Hunter leaned against the truck, hands still stuck in his pockets. He didn't look thrilled about the new development.

"Her name is Bailey," he said quietly, while not looking at her.

"Hi." She glanced between the two brothers.

The new one carried himself with so much more confidence. He kind of reminded her of Caleb.

"Fynn," said the brother and shook her hand firmly while flashing a straight, white smile.

Hunter made a noise, something like a snort, but covered it with a cough.

"So..." Bailey said, searching for conversation. "Little brother?"

Fynn laughed easily, letting his fingers linger on hers a bit too long. "Yes, Hunter is my younger brother. We have another brother, too, but he's at school."

"We have unpacking to do," Hunter said, pulling a lamp from the bed of the truck.

"I could help," Bailey said, purposely forgetting she was supposed to meet Charity for homework. She tossed her backpack on the ground in the corner.

The two brothers exchanged looks as Hunter set the lamp down hard on the cement and Fynn stepped between Bailey and the entrance to the house.

"No, thank you," Hunter said.

"We couldn't let you get dirty or hurt lifting something heavy," Fynn added.

Immediately, Bailey felt her face heat up. Because she was a girl and she might break a nail? She was about to let him have a piece of her mind, when she caught herself and forced another hopefully un-creepy smile.

"I'm not that fragile, I promise." She was proud of her decorum.

"Maybe when our mother's home," Hunter said, in his soft voice. "I don't think she'd want anyone to see the house until she's ready."

Bailey's ego deflated. That was reasonable, and she couldn't burn bridges when she had such an opportunity.

"I'll stop by tomorrow morning at eight," she said directly to Hunter. "And we can walk to school together. I can help you find your classes."

He may be a tougher nut to crack than his brother, but there was something about him that spoke to Bailey. Maybe it was his calm and quiet attitude, or that he didn't seem to care if he impressed anyone. Either way, she wouldn't mind getting to know him better, and she should at least have some genuine interest if she wanted to get close enough to this family to get into the house.

"That's okay," Hunter started to turn her down and Bailey's heart sank into her stomach.

"Too bad I'm not in high school anymore," Fynn interrupted, giving her a spark of hope, "or I'd take you up on that in a second.

Hunter will be ready at eight." He threw an arm over his brother's shoulder, nearly knocking him off his feet.

Bailey scooped up her bag and gave them a thumbs-up as she quickly backed off and down the path before Hunter had a chance to find an excuse. And as she looked back at the house, on her way down the street, she thought she saw movement again in the attic window, three stories up. Maybe their father was in the house? They'd already eluded to their other brother and mom being out. Either that or they were lying for some reason. But that was stupid, because what would a new family in town have to lie about?

Bailey was letting her imagination get the best of her. These people had nothing to do with the real mystery of the Gallows House. They hadn't known her brother.

They hadn't killed him.

CHAPTER 2

Charity pouted from the front stoop of the house. Bailey could make out her pink lips the minute she turned the corner. Her friend popped up and dashed toward her at the same time.

"You're late. I thought you got kidnapped or something."

Bailey shook her head as she fished the key from her pocket to let them inside the two-story which was half the size of the Gallows House. No one else seemed to feel it, but since Caleb died, Bailey felt as cold and repulsed in her own home as the latter. She hadn't been able to even tell that to Charity, though. It felt wrong, like she was betraying her father or something.

"Met some new neighbors," Bailey said, as they swung the door closed and tossed their bags down. They'd get to homework eventually.

"The Lees and Hagenmillers have lived here, like, forever." Charity scrunched her tiny nose beneath the large plastic pink frames of her glasses.

Bailey retrieved two glasses from the cupboard and fished in the fridge for the milk.

"Further down," she mumbled, pouring a good dose for each of them.

It hadn't escaped her notice that Charity automatically discounted the street she was on the corner of, or that she never walked home with Bailey, only met her there when specifically asked. It was like an avoidance spell on the house.

"You mean near the Gallows House?" Charity asked, working it out as she pulled the plate of fresh baked cookies—AKA her dad's attempt at parenting since her mother left—toward her at the breakfast bar.

"Closer," Bailey said, grabbing one of the oatmeal wonders from the plate.

"Closer? But…" Charity blinked and went a shade paler at the realization. "No way. Are you sure they were, you know, real?"

Bailey grinned, remembering the depth in Hunter's large eyes, and nodded.

"They have three boys. One's our age. His name's Hunter and I'm walking him to school tomorrow."

"Is he cute?" Charity asked, dunking her cookie.

That's what her first question was?

Bailey rolled her eyes. "Yeah, I guess. But if you're going for looks, his college-age brother is the one you want. His name is Fynn."

"I do like older men," Charity mused, over a mouthful of deliciousness.

"Anyway, it's perfect. We'll get to know Hunter, and pretty soon we'll have an all-access pass."

"Does that mean we can forget about the Halloween plan?" Charity asked hopefully.

Bailey thought for a moment. Did it? Halloween was the one night people sought out the Gallows House, especially people her age. She'd had it worked out for months. She would get a group together and bring a Ouija board over to the grounds, like it was a game. But while she was there, she could find a way to break in or dare someone else to do it. Then she'd have all night to search the house. Not that she knew what she was searching for exactly, but something deep inside told her the answers were there, beyond those impenetrable walls.

"Obviously we can't break in now." She sipped her milk. "But maybe we can get ourselves invited over for Halloween. Maybe we can convince Hunter he'd be the most popular guy in town if he had a party that night. Literally everyone would come."

The more she worked it out, the more excited she got. With all those people, she'd be totally free to explore the house without anyone noticing.

"A party there on Halloween?" Charity said, with something close to awe. "Brilliant."

"Why, thank you." Bailey grinned and offered her cookie in a toast.

***

Apparently, word spread quickly despite no one ever going down the street, because when Bailey arrived the next morning there were at least fifty people of various ages gawking at the Gallows House from about a hundred yards away. Bailey hesitated at the front of the walkway, feeling thoroughly awkward with all those people watching. As she stood, trying to figure out what to do, Fynn came out the front door, waving at her.

"Bailey, there you are." He rushed toward her and a murmur rose in the crowd.

Fynn seemed to like it though. He made sure to keep smiling and glancing over at the lot of them.

"Where's Hunter?" she asked, keeping her back to the crowd.

"He left out the back. Doesn't like crowds. If you hurry you can catch up."

Bailey nodded. She didn't blame him. She'd hate it, too. She *did* hate it. When all those curiosity seekers pretended to be longtime friends and *comfort* her when Caleb died, they were so obviously fake she figured she could knock them over like cardboard.

"They want to know who bought the house. They think it's haunted," she offered in way of thanks, before shuffling off down the block.

She heard him introducing himself to the closest onlookers as she moved on, scanning the street for signs of Hunter. He had such long legs she was afraid she may not be able to catch him. She needn't have worried though, because she found him staring up at a large knotted ash tree about a block from the corner of Willow and Oak. She moved to stand beside him and cranked her neck back toward the tree tops, hands tucked under the straps of her backpack. When she couldn't figure it out, she spoke up.

"What are we looking at?" she asked, watching the leaves rustle.

"It's weird," Hunter said softly, as though they'd been having a conversation all along. "The wind here comes from different directions at the same time. See how the leaves are moving?"

"Yeah." She noted the breeze that must've been coming from their left.

"Well, look at the tree next to us. It should be blowing, too, right?"

"I guess." Bailey shrugged.

She hadn't felt a breeze and she'd come from that way.

"Well, wind doesn't start at random spots between trees," Hunter said and furrowed his thick brown brows.

Bailey looked over to the left and saw that the movement of the leaves all made sense. Yet to the right, back toward the Gallows House, everything was absolutely still.

"Come on or we'll be late," Bailey said, then took his arm and steered him toward the school.

It wasn't the only weird thing he was bound to notice.

"I should probably warn you," she said as they approached the edge of the street. "You're gonna have a lot of people interested in you today, so be prepared for attention."

Hunter glanced down at her as their strides evened out.

"Because I'm new?"

"Nope. Because of where you live."

He nodded as though she'd just validated something he long suspected.

"That's why there was a crowd outside this morning? You spread the word, I guess."

Bailey stopped dead in her tracks, causing Hunter to spin around in confusion.

"I didn't do that."

She had to make friends with this guy, but she wouldn't let him insult her.

Hunter stared at her like she was as big a mystery as the strange wind. Bailey knew the minute they stepped around the corner the world would come into full, obnoxious focus, saturating their senses. She wasn't in a hurry for that.

"You didn't tell people we moved into the foreclosure," he said, after finally working it out.

"No," Bailey said, firmly.

Hunter sighed and adjusted his hat. "Well, I guess it would've gotten out eventually. Still, I didn't expect to be that much of an oddity. What's wrong with those people? Just because we don't have a lot of money doesn't mean—"

"It's not because of money," Bailey interrupted what she imagined to be his self-righteous tirade. "It's because of the house. It's haunted."

Hunter's confused expression morphed into one of mirth and he started to laugh. Bailey realized it was the first time she'd seen him smile. It looked good on him, even if his amusement was misplaced.

"You're serious," he said, still laughing.

"Yeah. I don't know what's in that place, but there *is* something there. Anyway, I thought you should know before we get to school." Bailey shifted, feeling uneasy under the intensity of his gaze.

Slowly, Hunter calmed down and shook his head. "All right. Thanks for the warning. But that isn't why you were hanging around yesterday, is it? Is that why you wanted to walk me to school? To get into the haunted house? Because you can go on ahead now if that's the case."

Bailey's face warmed again. "I was trying to be nice," she snapped.

Though he'd nailed it and it was exactly as awful as he made it sound. What had she been thinking? She still had to get in that house, but it wasn't right to use this guy to do it.

"Sorry," he said, stepping close enough for her pulse to speed up. "That was mean. I shouldn't assume the worst."

"Is that the worst you can assume?" she asked and they both laughed.

Bailey felt lighter as they continued on toward the school. And, for some reason, she didn't mind the sudden intensity of the sun or the sound of others' loud whispers as they headed toward the steps of Lincoln High. Walking with Hunter down Willow made the weird transition more bearable.

Bailey waited while Hunter got his schedule from the counseling office, and walked him to his first class. They had one period together—the last one—and Bailey was surprised to find herself excited about the possibility of walking back home with him.

CHAPTER 3

The house was all anyone talked about, all day long. Several people attempted to grill her because they'd heard she'd been there this morning and one of the new occupants knew her by name. Haunted house plus hot twenty-year-old was apparently more exciting than if the Olympics came to Shadow Springs.

But Hunter still managed to keep mostly to himself throughout the day, always in Bailey's periphery. Sure, there were gawkers and some bold people who approached him to talk, but he greeted them politely and went back to whatever he was doing.

When Bailey got to History and slipped into her seat near the back window, she was surprised to see Hunter come in and head directly for the open desk behind her. Charity, who was already seated at her side, gawked open-mouthed at Hunter, giving Bailey a thumbs-up as he settled in.

"Hi, I'm Charity."

Hunter barely glanced up as he muttered a tired sounding hello. Charity pouted.

"Charity's a good friend," Bailey said. "Charity, this is Hunter. So... how was your first day?"

"Okay, I guess," he said, leaning down with his chin resting on the back of her chair. "Tell me this attention thing will die down soon."

Bailey debated lying to make him feel better, but deemed herself too guilty for being less than honest earlier about her intentions.

"Probably not until after Halloween." She grimaced apologetically. "Your house is usually a hotspot for people on that day. And it's also kind of a big deal here. Halloween, I mean."

"Oh."

Bailey wanted to say the right thing to bring back his elusive smile, but the teacher started class and she was forced to face forward.

Mr. Klosky introduced Hunter from the roster, and everyone turned around as he waved a little before slinking down into his seat, his legs so long that his feet bumped the back of Bailey's orange high-tops.

"Being that it's October and I know all your heads will be filled with Halloween," Mr. Klosky said, mercifully changing the subject. Sort of. "I want you to split into groups of four and we will be picking subjects out of my trusty hat, each having to do with a supposed paranormal hotspot in and around Shadow Springs. You will then research the subject and write an essay on the real history that led to the legend. And before you start begging, yes, The Gallows House is of course in here. But it goes only to the lucky group that picks it."

Bailey's brain jerked into overdrive as she sprung her hand in the air.

"Bailey," Mr. Klosky called, as students prepared to group themselves together.

"Mr. Klosky, don't you think that subject should go to Hunter's group? Since it is his house now?"

She could feel his eyes burning a hole through the back of her head. She knew he didn't want any more attention. She also knew every person in the class was about to ask him to be a member of their team, and likewise every person in town already knew his address.

Mr. Klosky raised his eyebrows until they disappeared into his shaggy bangs, and his mouth dropped open. Maybe Bailey had miscalculated. Maybe Klosky was the last one to find out the gossip. Luckily, he recovered quickly and nodded.

"Thank you for pointing that out. Of course, that makes sense. Yes, Mr. Callahan's group should have that honor."

Bailey spun around and shot Hunter a coy look. "Sorry. I figured you'd rather not leave that to chance. You don't want some gawkers trying to harass you in your new place with this kind of excuse."

"Totally," Charity agreed, already pulling her desk toward them.

Hunter scowled. "Next time let me make that decision, please."

Bailey tried her best to look abashed, and he sighed, sitting up straight in his chair.

"I guess it makes sense," he said. "But there's only three of us. He said we need four."

No sooner did the words fall from his lips than the predators moved in. The entire class huddled around their desks, all talking at once and shoving forward.

A wave of protectiveness passed over Bailey as Hunter's face fell, and she stood on her seat, banging the window beside her with her orange shoe.

"Hey!" she yelled. "There's only room for one more in the group, so settle down. What are you, wild animals?"

Hunter slunk back down and stared at his pencil as he twirled it between his fingers.

"This is a person, not a circus entertainer. Pick a number one to one hundred and write it down. Hunter's going to pick a number and whoever can prove they have it, joins. Got it? Go."

Bailey watched, amused as they all scrambled for a scrap of paper and scribbled. When the dust settled, she leaned in toward Hunter.

He moaned and said, "Thirty-two?"

"Who has number thirty-two?" Bailey asked, standing up once again.

A girl in the back squealed, jumping up and down and waving her scrap of paper. Everyone else muttered, shot hostile looks at Bailey and Charity, and moved back to their seats to form other groups. The girl, who Bailey could now see was Leah Tucker, daughter of retired Hollywood starlet, Paula Tucker, pulled a chair over as close to Hunter as possible. So close, in fact, that her double-Ds brushed the outside of his arm.

"Hi, I'm Leah," she said directly to Hunter.

"Hey," he said, still staring at his rapidly moving pencil.

"Let's split up the work," Bailey said quickly. "Charity, you and Leah can research at the library. Hunter and I will see what we can find on the property."

"That's not fair," Leah pointed out. "I hate libraries. Besides, you and Charity already work well together. I'll go home with Hunter." She grabbed his elbow, laying claim.

Bailey's nostrils flared as the familiar heat flooded her face. This was her chance, finally, and she wasn't going to let Caleb down because of Leah throwing herself at Hunter.

"Why don't we all stick together?" Hunter said in his soft voice. "There's nothing at the house except our own stuff. I'm sure the town hall has records. We're more likely to find information there. Maybe we can also talk to the realtor that sold my mom the house."

"Smart and mysterious," Leah cooed. "And we think alike." She ran a long, manicured nail down his arm and bit her bottom lip.

"Think alike?" Hunter asked blankly.

"Thirty-two?" she prompted.

"Right," he said and twirled the pencil faster. "Why don't we start on our phones since we have the rest of the hour?"

"Charity is really good at that stuff," Leah offered, looking at the girl for the first time.

"Gee, thanks," Charity deadpanned, but pulled out her phone and started Googling. "The Gallows house has a long and sordid history," she began after a minute. "Built by Travis Randall Beckham in 1882, the house was initially the finest and largest in the town, but took on the tragic name of The Gallows House merely eight years later when, in a fit of grief, Beckham took—" Charity's mouth snapped shut, leaving them in silence.

"Took what?" Bailey prompted, annoyed.

Leah grabbed for her phone and her lined eyes grew wide as she read the rest.

"She didn't want to upset you, Bailey. But if it's too difficult, it's totally okay if you want to join another group."

Bailey's blood boiled. She wasn't going anywhere.

Charity grabbed her phone back and finished the sentence. "He took his own life by hanging himself in the front yard."

There was a heavy silence as Charity rubbed the back of her neck.

Hunter eyed Bailey with sad curiosity, and she hated him looking at her like that. He didn't need to know about the worst moment of her life. How *dare* Leah bring it up? So what if this old dude killed himself? It sounded like he actually had a reason. It was totally different.

"That's sad." Bailey shrugged like it was no big deal.

"And creepy," Leah said.

"Who was he grieving?" Bailey asked.

She hadn't found much when she'd looked. Then again, she wasn't particularly interested in the distant past. She was more concerned with recent history in her own investigations.

"It doesn't say any more on this site," Charity said, tucking stray strawberry-colored hair back behind her ear. "There is a book listed on Amazon, by Sean Tarlove. Should we order it?"

"Let's see if it's at the library first," Hunter said. "Then we won't have to wait or spend money on it."

"Let's go after school." Leah curled closer to Hunter, who stiffened in response.

So much for her hating libraries. In fact, Bailey found herself annoyed that Leah was making Hunter uncomfortable. What she'd said about Bailey's life was already over the line. But this was unacceptable. Bailey wanted to believe it was because she liked Hunter and wanted to help him escape all this fake attention that had plagued her not long ago. But she had to wonder if it was because Leah reminded her so much of her brother's ex, Amber, with her bouncy hair and hourglass figure. She couldn't deny the connection. No matter what the reason, she had a desire to poke something between Leah and Hunter's bodies and pry them apart.

"I don't have time today," Hunter said, staring down at the pencil between his long fingers. "I have to help unpack and do some repairs. We still have a lot to do."

"I can come help," Leah offered.

"No company until his mom feels the house is ready," Bailey said, maybe a little too quickly.

Hunter's face lifted in surprise, his eyes meeting hers with something like gratitude as a hint of the smile he'd let loose earlier played on his full lips.

"Oh," Leah said, clearly disappointed.

They exchanged cell numbers as the bell rang, and like Pavlov's dogs, everyone packed up and rushed for the door. As usual, Charity waved goodbye and headed in another direction. Bailey didn't blame her. She knew it was due to forces beyond her control. She was curious what would happen now that the Callahan family was on the entire town's radar. Would everyone take the turn down Willow or keep moving on down Oak? It seemed to Bailey that going by the Gallows House was a choice one had to make before one got to the corner.

Her train of thought was interrupted when she saw the same beat-up red pickup from the when she met Hunter. Fynn pulled up across from the school, leaned out the window and honked the horn, attracting the attention of everyone in a fifty-yard radius.

"Where's the best place for a break?" he shouted at anyone in earshot. "Just got off work and I want to have some fun before I get back to work on the house. Who's with me?"

A bunch of students and a few adults whooped, and someone shouted, "Molly's."

Bailey continued on past. She hadn't set foot in Molly's Ice Cream Shoppe since losing Caleb. He'd worked there for two years and she'd loved every minute she spent eating sundaes and laughing with all their friends. She could still picture him smiling from behind the counter, in his red and white checkered hat that clashed with whatever plaid shirt he wore that day.

Bailey pulled the open plaid shirt she wore now closer and leaned her face toward the shoulder where she could still barely pick up the faint smell of her brother's body spray. It had faded over time, but she was determined to keep every detail as real in her mind as the last time she'd seen him.

She'd been so wrapped up in memories she hadn't even noticed turning onto the quiet of Willow. And she was doubly surprised when someone laid a hand on her arm. So much so that her martial arts training from fifth grade kicked in and she pulled down and under, spinning with all her might, succeeding in yanking her assailant off balance. Both she and Hunter fell to the ground in a tumble of limbs. Bailey pushed up on her hands, staring down into Hunter's shocked face. He'd gotten the brunt of it, landing smack on his back over the sidewalk beneath her.

"Sorry." She righted herself into a sitting position.

Hunter accepted a hand to help him up, and rubbed the back of his head. He stooped to scoop up the cap that had fallen off his head, and Bailey admired his curly mop of dark hair while hoping she hadn't completely alienated him.

"I'll have to remember not to accidentally sneak up on you," he said softly. Then he rewarded her with a full-on grin.

Bailey's stomach did an unexpected little flip and she bent to hurriedly pick up their backpacks. Unfortunately, it was at the same moment he decided to do exactly that. She managed to bump heads with him and nearly knock him down again.

"I give," he said, backing off.

"Wait," she said, wanting him to stay put. "I'm glad you caught up with me."

So lame, but so true. For once, she wasn't content walking down the street alone.

Hunter stuck his hands in his pockets and waited for her to fall into step beside him.

"So…" Bailey glanced up at the trees to see if they were moving. They were still. Very still.

"Tell me more about Hunter Callahan."

She felt him shut down and tighten up, almost like when Leah brushed against him.

"I mean," she added quickly, "unless you want to hear more about me first. But that seems pretty boring. You know, born and raised. What you see is what you get."

"No skeletons in your closet?" he asked, bumping her a little.

She stumbled but regained her rhythm. "Not even a haunted house."

Though she'd found herself hoping many times this past year to feel her brother's presence. Eventually, she'd taken matters into her own hands by spending time in his room and wearing his favorite shirts on a regular basis.

"Well, I'm not convinced mine is haunted," Hunter said. "It's big and I can see why people think it's creepy, but I suspect when we get it all fixed up and filled with the smell of my mom's cooking, all that will magically disappear."

"So, you don't believe in ghosts?"

Bailey wasn't sure exactly what she believed. She knew something was there—something that had made her brother take his own life. Was it a ghost? Or was it something else? A curse? Was there a scientific explanation? She didn't know, and she was open to anything if it made sense.

Hunter shrugged. "I figure there's enough to be worried about in the world. There are worse things out there already, you know?"

Bailey nodded, fighting back the sorrow threatening to overtake her as the memory once again attempted to consume her. Waking up to the sudden, too-loud pop of the gun. Silence, then screaming from her mother. Her father's strong arms catching her around the waist to prevent her from getting to Caleb.

The white sheet over him with the dark red spot pooling larger and larger through the thin material, and the indentation where his head should've filled out the sheet.

"Are you okay?"

Hunter's voice was louder and held more emotion than she'd heard from him yet, and she realized he was a breath away. Long fingers grasped her arms. She could smell the faint traces of Caleb and home cooking, and despite the warmth and comfort of her brother's old shirt and Hunter's gaze, she felt suddenly dreadfully dizzy.

"Yeah," she replied. "Yeah of course. Why? What happened?"

She realized she couldn't remember them pausing their walk or conversation, nor him coming so close.

"You stopped and got really pale. You started swaying and I was worried you might pass out." Hunter's voice was deep and soft like a warm blanket, gently wrapping around her.

"Sorry. I guess I got lost in thought. I didn't mean to scare you." She waited because she didn't entirely want him to let go or move away.

"No offense," Hunter said, doing exactly that. "But I know when someone's keeping secrets—and it's cool."

"It's cool?" she asked, wiping at her eyes because they itched from unshed tears.

"Yeah. You don't know me, and obviously I don't know you. There's no reason you owe me anything, even an explanation. I do appreciate your help earlier, though. Fending off the wolves."

"No problem."

A heavy sadness settled over her because of his words. He was right, though. They didn't know each other. All the same, she felt comfortable with him and she'd hoped he felt the same with her. He could be an ally in her search for the truth.

Hunter paused at the edge of the lawn in front of the great willow tree.

"You want me to walk you the rest of the way?" he asked, glancing back at the house like it was calling to him.

"I can make it," Bailey assured him. "I'm a big girl."

"Yeah. You can always knock 'em down." Hunter gave an awkward shove against her arm.

Bailey saluted him and started down the rest of the street. She was past the next house when she heard him.

"Aren't there ever any birds around here?"

Bailey stopped. She glanced left and then right. There wasn't a single crow or songbird in sight. Not a chirp or a shuffle. Not even an ant on the sidewalk, come to think of it.

She spun back to face him. "I never noticed."

She sounded disturbed, and she was. How could she not have noticed that before? Or the wind thing he pointed out earlier?

A whistle pierced the air and Hunter pulled his phone from a pocket in his baggy jeans.

"Gotta go," he said. "My mom needs some help and my brother isn't home yet."

Bailey nodded and waved, then headed off once again toward her own home and her own ghosts.

CHAPTER 4

Charity had a family thing, which left Bailey alone in the house. Naturally, she headed straight for Caleb's room. She was the only one who'd used it since he died. Their mother basically broke when it happened, and left them and the house full of memories behind. Their father stayed and did the best he could for her, but worked crazy hours as his own way to cope. So the literal mess Caleb left behind still littered the floor, except for the few shirts she'd commandeered. The original mattress and bedding were long gone though, removed along with the rest of Caleb, and replaced with a cheap, quick shopping trip a few months later.

Bailey lay on her back, hair splayed over the pillow and arms wrapped around a cluster of his T-shirts, in the hopes of conjuring his presence. Staring at the unmoving ceiling fan, she allowed the well she'd been holding behind her eyes to finally leek untethered now that she was out of Hunter's sight. She wondered what Caleb would've thought about the Callahans moving into the Gallows House.

After she'd shed all the tears she was able to, Bailey got up and sat at Caleb's desk then pulled out the corkboard she had hidden beneath. She carefully placed it on top of the blotter and the back of the framed picture of Amber she had toppled over after being unable to look at it any longer. He'd loved her and she hadn't only abandoned him, but accused him as well. Bailey still couldn't bring herself to get rid of it altogether since he had felt so strongly for her.

"We have some new information to add," she announced.

She liked to talk out loud when no one was home, assuming Caleb was there watching and unable to answer for reasons she couldn't understand. She ran a finger over her brother's smiling senior portrait in the center of the board, and glanced over at the thick line connecting him to a picture of the Gallows House and a copy of his obituary. She plucked out a couple index cards and a

Sharpie from the top drawer. On one she wrote, *No wildlife in proximity*. On the other she wrote, *Wind stops suddenly only on street*. She then secured them with push pins near the picture of the house pinned among a cluster of other cards, scraps of paper, and sticky notes.

With a heavy sigh, she laid it on the top of the bed and paced back and forth in front of it.

"What do we know?" she asked Caleb. "We know you were happy. You had a life plan, an early college acceptance, and a girlfriend who claims you snapped on her the night you did this." She pressed a hand to her forehead, rubbing away the stress headache starting there. "We know you visited the house that night, and something happened there that made Amber run in tears and claim you attacked her." The words felt heavy in her throat and she fought to get through them. "I *know* you didn't. You couldn't. But we have to take that into account," she said, imagining Caleb silently angered and arguing his innocence. "So, what happened that night? Was it a ghost? A demon? A curse? Or was it a chemical that made you go insane? Maybe Amber lied and you felt there was no other way out." She winced, hating that she'd even said it.

She didn't doubt Amber was lying about something. She also knew her brother would never give up that easily. He was a fighter, not a quitter.

More confused than ever, she took the corkboard and put it back under the desk. Then she powered on the computer and searched for lack of animals and wind, but found nothing valuable. Of course, when she added *haunting* to the search, tons of pages came up.

"This is so frustrating!" she yelled, and powered down to leave the room.

She was on her way out, when she heard something above her and looked up to find the fan slowly moving. Bailey frowned. *What the heck?* She watched as it sped up to the point that her hair and all the loose papers in the room began to shift. One of the papers flittered across the floor and landed at her feet. As she picked it up, the fan began to slow to a full stop. The paper trembled, along with her fingers as she scanned for clues. It was an old history paper with an "A" scrawled across the top in red ink. She collapsed on the floor, sobbing when she read the title.

The Gallows House.

It was the paper her group was supposed to work on, dated two years prior. But as she read through tear-blurred eyes, she found nothing of consequence. It was the first page and had little she didn't already know.

Every small town may have a haunted house, but Shadow Springs's haunted house's validity is the one thing everyone in town agrees upon. And like all good haunted houses, the Gallows House's story began with death and tragedy.

The rest was a repeat of the information Charity had read off the Internet earlier. Travis Beckham had hung himself after suffering a string of tragedies, starting with his first wife's death mere months after the house was completed. And then nothing. The rest of the report was no longer attached.

In a fit of desperation, Bailey tore through the mess on the floor, searching for the rest of the story. She stopped when she got all the way across to the desk and put her face in her hands.

"I'm sorry, Caleb. I feel like I'm failing you. I still don't get it."

Another sound behind her made her turn, ready to run, but all she saw was the door to the closet slightly ajar. Had it been like that before? She scrambled to her feet and walked into the closet, pulling the worn plaid shirt closer to keep off the sudden chill.

Not knowing what she was looking for, she searched more methodically this time, until she reached the shoe boxes on the bottom. She was about to give up, when she found a small brown book stuck in between the boxes. She pulled it out as the light in the room blinked.

It had to be the book Charity had mentioned earlier. *The Gallows House: A West Coast Haunting.* The thin paperback was dogeared and worn, with sentences highlighted and marked with quick notes in Caleb's handwriting throughout.

Excitement flowed through her as she realized the potential importance of what she held in her hands. Hadn't she been asking Caleb for help in figuring out what happened when he died? She'd yelled about how frustrating it was that she couldn't find anything. This had to be him showing her the way.

"Thank you." she said, holding it against her chest.

For the first time in months, she felt hopeful about solving Caleb's death.

Bailey ran back to her room to start reading. Caleb had finally shown himself and she was thrilled. He really *was* with her and he *wanted* her to do this.

The Gallows House: A West Coast Haunting
by
Sean Tarlove

Pg. 13

Beckham soon met the only daughter of local politician Brett Carlton, and promptly fell in love with the sweet, spunky girl of barely sixteen. Rumor has it, he managed to procure her hand in marriage by promising to build the "greatest mansion California has ever seen" as a wedding present to her and all their future heirs. Carlton couldn't say no if Travis was offering to share his great and quickly accumulated wealth with his own family. After all, Travis had no one else to share it with, and it would come in handy for future runs for office.

By all accounts, Eugenia was thrilled with the prospect of being the envy of so many, especially since she was a social butterfly who loved hosting parties and other events. Sadly, she would succeed in doing so only twice before becoming bedridden with the illness that would claim her life before the tender age of seventeen, leaving her father without a way into Beckham's pockets, and Travis heartbroken and without an heir.

Did he know yet? Check blueprint originals.

Pg. 18

Though Beckham continued his habit of moving forward at a fast pace, the death of his first wife, Eugenia, had to have been like a bullet to the strongman's heart. Eugenia's was the first death recorded in what was supposed to be her dream home and the beginning of a future together with her new husband. Those close to the couple knew something was terribly wrong when Eugenia quarantined herself to her rooms on the second floor of the mansion, based on her typically outgoing and social attitude which rivaled her husband's.

It wasn't until Travis announced her death that anyone allowed themselves to believe it, however. The town doctor, Jerome Wilde, signed the death certificate, saying she died of influenza on

February 28, 1883, a mere month prior to her seventeenth birthday. Because of fears of contagion at the time, Eugenia had a quick, small funeral for those closest to the family, but Beckham spared no expense at laying her to rest in the finest comfort he could bestow on his loving bride.

Check records.

Pg. 23
    Though Travis Randall Beckham's life was filled with tragedy, including his three wives all dying in the supposed dream house he designed and built from the ground up, it wasn't until his own death that the curse—and name—of the Gallows House was born.
    Some believe it was Eugenia, Maureen, and Katherine Beckham who set the curse in motion. Some say Travis's wives were also cursed, starting with Eugenia's illness, escalating with Maureen being trampled by her own horse, and ending for the Beckham women with Katherine's ill-fated fall down the stairs. Whatever the truth, Beckham's final act of hanging himself from his favorite spot, the willow in the front yard, was the act that triggered the reports of spirits claiming residence in the home.

Who is the ghost? More than one?

CHAPTER 5

The groupies outside the Callahan's property got stranger every morning instead of dissipating. Although the numbers stayed to less than thirty, they were always gone by the time Bailey and Hunter returned home in the afternoon, their plastic chairs and fast food wrappers left behind like an abandoned campsite. It was like the combination of Halloween and people moving into the most haunted house in town had led to a bizarre reality TV show, of which the Callahans were the unwitting stars. Bailey's stomach hurt when she considered that people were gathering in the hopes of something terrifying happening to someone else, especially Hunter's family.

This particular morning, there was an actual camera crew, complete with a journalist in suit and tie. Bailey walked closer than usual so she could make out what he was asking the hippy-looking woman in front of him. The sight of Hunter leaning into the shadow of a tree about a house-length down caught her attention. He always escaped out back unnoticed, and waited for her to catch up. They'd noted over and over again during the past couple of weeks how weird it was that no one seemed to notice or care about anything outside of a tight radius around the house.

"… a real life medium. So, Ms. Capote, you speak with the dead?" the man with the microphone asked, seemingly bemused.

"That's right. Spirits speak through me," the woman said, in a voice that was far too high and breathy.

"Can you talk to the ghosts in the Gallows House? What is it they want? Is the family currently occupying the home safe?"

He tipped the microphone capped in an unnecessary wind guard toward her as she shut her blue lidded eyes to concentrate.

Bailey nearly tripped on a crack in the sidewalk where a root had taken hold because she was so focused on the conversation. She wondered if this woman was for real.

"There are several energies here," she whispered. "Mostly women, a couple men, all young to middle aged."

"Could one of them be Mr. Beckham, the builder of the house?"

"The oldest is a dark spirit," she continued as though she hadn't heard him. She scrunched her eyes. "It sees me."

"Is it him?"

The woman's breaths came fast and shallow as she clutched a black crystal on a chain laying between her breasts.

"No. I command you to stop. I *banish* you."

Bailey stopped and watched with full attention now. Would the evil spirit listen? Was this nothing but a show?

The woman grew more and more agitated as she muttered what sounded like Latin.

The reporter glanced toward the cameraman. "There you have it, folks. A real haunted house right here in southern California. Thank you, Ms. Capote. Now, back to you in the studio, Jeff."

He made the throat-slicing motion with his hand and dropped the mic to his side, but the woman was still battling internally with something, until her eyes burst open and she screamed.

"We already cut to the news," the reporter said over his shoulder, like he thought she was acting.

But Bailey didn't think that. Not when she dropped her hand and held it out by the wrist, like it burned. Tiny pebbles of stone rained out from her palm to the ground, and the chain that had held the crystal she clutched was empty.

Bailey ran to her and grabbed her wrist to examine the damage. Tiny bits of dark crystal glistened, embedded in her hand, while dots of blood bloomed from a thousand tiny wounds.

The woman pulled her hand back and wrapped it in a scarf pulled from her hair.

"It'll be okay," she said, more to herself than to Bailey.

"What *happened*?" Bailey asked, incensed that no one else had come to aid the woman in such obvious trouble.

"Stay away from this house," the woman said, voice deeper and less breathy than in the interview. "It can cause bodily harm."

"Come on, Bailey," Hunter said. "We have to get to school."

He tugged her arm and she whipped around, surprised he'd ventured toward the crowd, but quickly turned back to the medium.

"Wait, is he in danger?" Bailey asked, gesturing to Hunter. "His family? Did it hurt Caleb? Is that what happened?"

She could hear herself becoming more and more frantic as she begged for information.

As Hunter tugged her away, the medium's eyes fluttered shut again, eyes moving rapidly beneath her colorful lids. When she opened them again, Bailey was sure they'd changed color. Was it the morning light filtering through the trees, or were they red? The woman smiled in a way that made Bailey's heart stick in her throat.

"Caleb didn't cooperate," she said in a low voice.

This time it was too low to be natural, though still as soft as Hunter's. Then her eyes closed again and the medium collapsed on the ground.

"Oh, my God, someone call an ambulance," Bailey shrieked, pulling away from Hunter's grasp.

Had he even heard that? Had he seen her change like that?

Bailey turned to grab him by the T-shirt and tried to shake him.

"Calm down, Bailey," he said, in a quiet, calming way that actually helped. "She's okay. Look."

He turned her around, hands on her shoulders, to find the woman climbing to her feet and dusting herself off. She seemed confused but not harmed as she moved away from them, back toward the crowd.

"Wait, I need to know more," Bailey called.

But the woman hurried further away without a glance back. Finally, Bailey gave up and turned to Hunter, letting her face fall against his surprisingly solid chest. She beat her forehead against him like he was a wall, and after a few seconds he enfolded her into an awkward hug.

When she straightened up, she tugged at his shirt again, trying to get out the wrinkles and damp spot she'd left behind, not appreciating the evidence left from her losing her composure once again.

Hunter merely gave her a small smile. "Let's go," he said, and led the way toward Oak. Bailey was used to the silence between them at this point, as neither one seemed to want to give up their secrets. However, it had become comfortable. Even desired. But right now, her head was ready to implode with the scene she'd witnessed. It would help if Charity were there to talk it through.

She was so tempted to break down and tell Hunter everything. He was so levelheaded and calm. Maybe he'd see something she hadn't. Then again, he still hadn't had her—or anyone else—come any closer than the front sidewalk. He talked about his mom and her cooking, but Bailey had never met the woman or his youngest brother, Tom.

Sure, Fynn always seemed to be nearby and had luckily taken the brunt of socializing off his brother, but he was only about the moment. He'd be suave about it, even flirtatious, then he'd change the subject as quickly as Hunter did when confronted with questions regarding the house and their family.

"Halloween is coming up." Bailey eyed a car at the corner of Oak that had a fake arm hanging out of the trunk.

"Yeah," Hunter replied.

As usual, the breeze and noise picked up the second they turned.

"Has anyone asked about visiting the house for Halloween?" she asked, then held her breath.

Hunter narrowed his eyes at her and shrugged. "I think they've mostly asked Fynn. He's much better at letting people down nicely."

"Because it's sort of a tradition to bring a Ouija board and candles to the property and try to sneak in. I'm saying this because I want to warn you that I'm guessing people will try, no matter what."

Hunter stopped at the bottom of the steps to the big brick school and searched Bailey with his eyes, as though he had X-ray vision and could discern her motive for saying all that. Bailey swallowed, praying he couldn't, because she was just as determined as before he moved in to get into that house. Especially after reading through the book and Caleb's notes. And well, now that the Medium had said what she did, Bailey had no choice. No matter what, she was getting in that house by Halloween.

"You want to come over, don't you?" Hunter crossed his arms. "For Halloween. Just like the rest of them."

Bailey knew she was blushing. "Are you inviting me?" she asked, with way more confidence than she felt.

"No." Hunter turned toward the steps as the late bell rang.

Bailey stayed put at the bottom, feeling nailed to the floor in her neon green high-tops.

Hunter stopped at the top and yelled down at her, "I plan to invite Charity and Leah, too, so it's not only you. I figured we could get some actual photos to use in the report. But no Ouija boards, okay?"

Bailey stayed glued to the ground as he disappeared through the doors.

That stinker. But Leah? Really? Ugh.

The Gallows House: A Westcoast Haunting
by
Sean Tarlove

Pg. 34

The first known murder to happen in the house was that of a young woman named Ingrid Blunt, who was, perhaps not coincidentally, the first girl of marrying age to move into the house since the Beckham tragedy.

Ingrid's older siblings were trusted with her estate after the untimely death of her parents. After her brother moved into town with his new wife, he gifted Ingrid the Gallows House, along with an announcement that he had arranged a marriage for her to a successful banker and widower, Tyler Parnell. Enraging her siblings, Ingrid took the house, but instead accepted an engagement to traveling salesman, Mr. Marshall Barnett, in the Spring of 1902. Ingrid openly stated that she chose true love and planned to live happily ever after.

Unfortunately for her, Ingrid's choice was an unstable one at best. While visiting to discuss wedding plans one Sunday afternoon, Mr. Barnett apparently snapped for some unknown reason and attacked his devoted fiancée with a butcher's knife. Her body was found on the second-floor landing, where she'd apparently crawled from her bedroom in an attempt to escape her attacker. Based on police and coroner reports, her body was nearly unrecognizable when it was found.

After Mr. Barnett finished with the attack, he climbed to the roof of the house, and, still covered in his beloved's blood, jumped, succeeding in snapping his spine. He spent the remainder of his days as an invalid at a nearby mental institution. He's reported to have stated that he did not remember hurting Ingrid and that he awoke to the spirit of a woman hovering over her body, and his own hands soaked in her blood.

Whose ghost? Was she responsible? Did he really not remember?

Pg. 42

In the winter of 1928, Artemis and Teresa Murphy moved into the Gallows House after buying it from an elderly man named Steven Dole. Artemis and Teresa spent money like water and had many a rowdy party at the mansion and grounds. When the great depression hit, it hit the Murphys hard as well, and the parties came to a stop. Artemis and Teresa reportedly fought quite a bit during those first couple of years, and when she became pregnant with a baby thought to belong to a local judge, Artemis strangled her to death, which also killed the unborn child. He was sentenced to life in prison.

Why didn't the curse strike sooner? Because they were depressed and angry?

CHAPTER 6

Afternoons became a comfortable habit of falling into step with Hunter as they made their way toward Willow. The weather was beginning to cooperate, too, cooling down enough for Bailey to wear Caleb's shirts without being uncomfortable. The leaves coordinated with the Halloween color scheme by turning shades of orange, brown, and red.

They were about to make the turn, when a familiar red pickup pulled right in front of them and squealed to a halt, making Hunter and Bailey dance backward for fear of being run over. The passenger side window rolled down and Fynn leaned over with his mischievous grin, dark hair slicked back, and gold-framed sunglasses pulled down below the bridge of his nose so his own chocolate eyes were visible.

"Hi, Bailey. How are you? How come I never see you stop by anymore?"

"Could be because you're never home," Hunter said before Bailey could open her mouth.

Fynn threw his head back and laughed like it was a great joke. "Touché, little bro. Well, I've decided that it's your turn to take a break from the double H's of hell and have a little fun."

Bailey dipped her eyebrows. "What are the double H's of hell?"

"He means housework and homework," Hunter muttered, obviously none too happy about his brother's sudden appearance.

Bailey understood instantly. Hunter wasn't as social as his brother. He didn't like being in the presence of a bunch of gawking people, and that seemed to be what Fynn thrived on.

"We're good, thanks," Bailey said, attempting to pull Hunter around the pickup.

Fynn threw the car into gear and backed up to remain in their way.

"No chance. Get in. Both of you." He reached over and swung the door open.

"Kidnapping is a federal offense," Bailey said.

"Maybe you'll let me bribe you with ice cream and change your mind about turning me in. Either way, I'll take my chances."

Hunter peered over the roof like he could see the house from where they stood.

"She's working late," Fynn said, "and we'll pick Tom up from school on the way. Consider it a fun family outing." He sounded less mischievous and far more like a concerned older brother.

Bailey's heart knocked on her chest and she shifted, checking out Hunter's expression, which was dubious.

"You should take a break," she said to Hunter.

Besides, she'd get to meet brother number three. Not that she was keen on going to Molly's. It would be the first time without Caleb behind the counter, but she supposed she'd have to face it sometime or another.

"Great, now it's two against one." Hunter sighed heavily as he gestured for Bailey to climb in first, then followed her up into the truck.

It was definitely high off the ground and slightly awkward being sandwiched between the two brothers. One side of her smelled like home-baked cookies, the other like aftershave, and the mix was unsettling to her stomach. She slunk down into the worn leather seat and pulled the collar of the blue and green plaid shirt up over her nose from either side so she could drown it all out with Caleb.

"Where's Tom gonna sit?" Bailey asked as she jolted first into one brother, then the other with every bump they hit.

It was a reasonable question, since they took over the entire bench and the rear was filled with tools, tires, and other random car parts.

"There's room in the back," Fynn said. "He can squeeze."

"I'll sit in the back," she offered when they pulled up to the middle school.

"I'll come with you." Hunter helped her down and then back up by hanging on to her waist as she climbed.

She noted a smaller version of what looked like a cross between Hunter and Fynn rushing over toward the truck. Tom's hair was long like Hunter's, and tucked beneath a baseball cap. His mouth and eyes, though, were shaped more like Fynn's. No telling yet if he was going to end up lanky like Hunter or not, as from the looks of it, he was still a head shorter than Bailey.

Hunter grabbed him into an affectionate hug and shoved his cap down over his face before climbing into the back with Bailey.

"Who's the babe?" Tom asked, standing on the edge of the truck so his head peeked over the side.

Bailey felt a blush burning her cheeks. "My name's Bailey, not babe."

"Hi, Bailey. Nice to meet you." Tom stuck out a hand.

She couldn't keep from smiling as she shook it.

"Are you with Fynn or Hunter?" he asked, making her balk again.

"She's a friend of both of ours, so talk to her with respect," Fynn said as Tom finished climbing in and closed the door. Neither of the two in the rear had settled into any kind of a seat when Fynn hit the gas and they ended up falling into the center of a giant tire with their legs up in the air. Hunter beat against the back window, which only succeeded in making his brother hit the gas harder.

Bailey squealed as things slid by them and ducked into Hunter's armpit, making him laugh uproariously.

"What's so funny?" she demanded, disentangling herself enough to peer out at him.

It was worse than a rollercoaster with loose machinery on board and no seatbelts.

"I didn't think you were afraid of anything, but it looks like I was wrong," Hunter said with a straight face.

"It's not fear, it's common sense," Bailey corrected, though she had to admit, now that they were moving steadily it wasn't so bad. Especially with Hunter so close and so… carefree. She liked him like that.

"You have a nice smile," Hunter said in his quiet voice, staring at her intently. "You should do it more often."

Funny, she'd been thinking the same thing about him.

"So, what's all this stuff doing in your brother's trunk?" she asked after a moment of silence.

Hunter shrugged. "Probably from the shop. He's been working at a mechanic down on Pine since we moved here."

"Oscar's? No way."

She knew Oscar well. He'd been a good friend of her dad's since high school. Of course, her dad had gone off to USC and come back with her mom, while Oscar had stayed and taken over the family business.

"Small town," Hunter said.

And she realized, for the first time, that at some point he'd worked his arm back around her waist, elbow resting on the rubber of the tire they occupied.

Bailey leaned her head on his shoulder. "What does your mom do?"

Hunter's muscles tensed beneath her, but only for a moment. "She's working at a hotel out in Lancaster, at the front desk."

"That's quite a distance," Bailey said, pulling back to look at him.

No wonder she seemed to be MIA so often.

"What about your dad?"

Hunter let out a heavy breath through his nose, but his hand remained in place around her. Before he could answer, the truck swerved right into a parking spot, and jolted to a stop. Hunter's grip on her waist tightened protectively until his brother's face appeared over the edge. Then his arm was gone like it had never been there.

Fynn offered a hand from the opposite side, and Bailey let him help her down. Before she could make the last jump, he grabbed her waist and hoisted her down, letting her slide along the front of him so their bodies touched the entire way. When she got to the ground, he held her in place for another moment, eyes locked on hers in a way that made her breath catch.

She'd never had a guy be this blatant about physicality. Sure, before Caleb's death she'd kissed a few guys and held hands. Nothing serious. Not that *this* was serious, just... intense, and she didn't know how she should react. Her body seemed to tingle in places that embarrassed her, but she focused her mind on Hunter, who was coming from the back of the truck, after having climbed down the other side.

Bailey pulled away, hugging herself. It had only been seconds, but it felt like an eternity until she'd made the decision, and for some reason she felt guilty about that.

Hunter watched her curiously. She couldn't tell what he'd seen or what he was thinking.

Tom rushed around the side of the truck. "Bailey. Have you ever been to Molly's? It's awesome. Fynn took me here last week and promised we'd come back. You have to try the caramel-triple-fudge sundae."

Bailey laughed as he opened the door for her. "Yeah, I've been here once or twice."

"Bailey's lived here her whole life. I think."

Hunter put a hand on her shoulder and she relaxed a little. He wasn't upset, at least.

"Yep," Bailey agreed, following Tom to the counter to grab some of the padded red stools.

The place was a study of red and white, and smelled like heaven. She had missed it, she realized, as the oldies pumped through the stereo system. Tom was already up on a stool, twirling in circles as fast as possible, as Hunter straddled the one between them with his long legs. Surprisingly, Fynn took the stool on her left instead of the one on the other side of Tom, and she knew he was leaning close based on the heat of his body.

"Fynn!" a blonde girl behind the counter screamed as though Christmas had come early, and she rushed toward him.

"Hey, Sam," Fynn said, less enthusiastically.

"How's your head feeling?" she asked, leaning across the bar area like she wanted to climb in his lap.

"What? Oh, much better, thanks. I just needed some caffeine." Fynn gestured at Bailey and the others. "Give these folks whatever they want and put it on my tab."

Sam moved over to start with Tom's order, a Banana Bomb, which was like a supersized banana split with sparklers on top. If the customer finished it, their picture went on the wall of fame and they earned a Molly's Champion T-shirt.

"Bomb," Sam yelled over her shoulder, and a guy came out whooping and hollering.

But when he set eyes on Bailey, he stopped in mid-whoop.

"Bailey. Man, it's been ages. I'm so glad you finally came back in."

Max's easy smile brought a pang to Bailey's heart. Memories of him and Caleb goofing around to make her laugh brought a melancholic mixture of emptiness and happiness she wasn't ready for.

"Hi, Max," she said, staring down at the paper placemat in front of her. "Just showing the new neighbors the town."

"You know each other?" Fynn asked, looping an arm over Bailey's shoulder. "Bailey, you've been holding out on me. You're going to have to come out with us this weekend and show me who else you know."

"Actually, we have a report to work on," Hunter said.

Bailey raised her head to find his intense eyes staring right at her.

"All weekend?" Fynn asked.

"Yep," Hunter replied. "It's a big report. Worth, like, fifty percent of our grade."

"School," Fynn muttered, releasing Bailey from his embrace. "Glad I'm done with that waste. And I probably make more as a mechanic than if I had to pay back a million loans to be some stuffy stockbroker or some shit."

"You're an assistant," Hunter said, under his breath.

"You work your way up, little bro. Isn't that right, Bailey?"

At this point, Bailey wanted nothing more than to go home and cuddle up on Caleb's bed, with his purple shirt. He'd been accepted to UCLA, his dream school, along with Amber. He saw college as a future worth having. How did Bailey feel? She'd have to start applying soon if she wanted to go somewhere, but she couldn't see herself leaving Shadow Springs, not without figuring out what happened to Caleb. She'd thought about being a detective. Maybe it would help her solve the mystery. But she didn't want to give up the years it would take to train. Maybe she'd search for online courses later.

"Hey, you okay?" Fynn nudged Bailey, and for once his bravado and charm were toned down enough to look genuinely concerned.

What did that mean she looked like?

"I'm fine," she said. "Just remembered some things I have to do at home." She slipped off the stool and waved goodbye to Max.

"I'll take you home," Fynn said, digging in his pocket, presumably for a wallet.

"No. No, you stay here. I like walking, and it isn't really that far. No more than a mile if I cut through a few yards." Bailey grinned.

"I'll walk you home." Hunter jumped up beside her. "I have some homework to do."

"Hey," Fynn said. "I thought we were having some family bonding time."

"Next time, check with me before," Hunter said. "I'll try to fit it in my schedule." His face was so straight, Bailey wasn't sure if he was joking or not. Either way, he led the way to the door and held it open for her.

"Come back soon, Bailey. I miss Caleb, but I miss you too," Max yelled, making her pause and cringe in the doorway.

Bailey managed a wave and some semblance of a smile before following Hunter outside. She began walking at such a fast pace that even with his long legs, Hunter had to hurry to catch up. The further she got from Molly's, the less thin the air felt and the easier she could breathe.

"Whoa, can we slow down a bit?" Hunter asked, keeping pace. "What happened back there? Wait, let me guess. You secretly hate ice cream?"

Bailey stopped walking about halfway down the street near the first houses, and started laughing so hard tears filled her eyes and she doubled over, clutching her knees. Hunter sat cross-legged on the edge of the nearest lawn and waited, picking at the crabgrass. She could barely see him through her tear-warbled vision, but she thought he looked awfully patient and calm despite her crazy breakdown.

Eventually, she was able to stop the laughing/crying fit, and sat down next to him before collapsing back onto the cool grass and pressing the heels of her hands against her closed eyes. She felt him lie next to her, and when she finally removed her hands and turned her head, there he was, inches away, staring at her with an infinite sort of patience.

"Sorry," she said.

The last thing she liked to do was break down in front of people.

"If you keep it bottled up long enough, it's bound to explode. At least that's what my mother keeps warning me about. Did she hire you by chance? You know, to show me what she's talking about?"

Bailey shook her head. "Your mom is a smart lady, but I haven't accepted any bribes lately. Maybe she really does know what she's talking about."

"Maybe you simply need the right person to help you unbottle it." Hunter shrugged, which looked surprisingly easy despite lying on the grass.

"If this is what unbottled looks like, most people would probably run screaming." Bailey sat up and let out a long breath.

Her legs shook slightly so she didn't try standing yet.

"I'm still here." Hunter sat up beside her and stretched his legs out across the width of the sidewalk.

"Indeed," Bailey agreed, knocking him with her shoulder. "And based on your mom's wisdom, I take it you have your own issues stored under pressure, in a glass container."

"I thought we were discussing your issues." Hunter raised one bushy eyebrow.

"No, we're discussing hypothetical bottles."

"Well, your hypothetical bottle had a leak. Therefore, I think we should focus on you."

"*Au contraire*," Bailey said, working her way to standing and offering him a hand. "Now some of the pressure's been released for me. Basic physics. You're in much more danger of a hypothetical blow up."

"Hypothetically, I suppose." Hunter kept hold of her hand as they walked toward home, taking the long way.

Bailey's pulse thudded when she thought about the way his large hand encompassed hers. Somehow he remained firm yet tender at the same time. To her surprise, it felt natural.

After a few blocks of watching the houses, birds, and trees, along with jack-o-lanterns—both childlike and intricately carved—Hunter finally spoke.

"Who's Caleb, Bailey?"

Maybe it was that he kept looking straight ahead and not at her. Or maybe it was the pressure release from that afternoon. Or maybe it was the way he continued to hold her hand like he expected her not to run away. But she answered him.

"He was my brother."

The words hung in the air, feeling as thick as when she'd spoken them.

"When?" Hunter asked, after a moment.

"January. He… they say he took his own life."

It was getting hard to breathe again.

"Did he?" Hunter asked, pulling her over to the shady side of the street beneath a large canopy of oaks.

"He pulled the trigger, only it wasn't him."

The words were fierce now, like knives that cut at her throat, but they were also harder to stop.

"I know how that sounds, okay? But I also know Caleb. He was ecstatic about going away to school. He had a girlfriend, and yeah, they had an issue that night, but he was always the logical thinker. He would've waited and made her talk it out. He wouldn't have acted irrationally like that. He just wouldn't."

Hunter nodded slowly, peering at the trees. It was exactly the right thing to do. He *got* it, and a huge weight lifted from her shoulders.

"My dad left when I was seven," he said, still staring up at the rustling leaves. "He left my mom with a ton of debt and three kids because his parents disowned him for marrying someone like her and, apparently, he lied when he said money didn't matter. Then he robbed a bank and got locked up for killing a policeman."

"Shit," Bailey said, after a moment of silence.

"Yeah. That about sums it up."

Hunter tugged her hand, and they continued along in silence.

"Is that why you moved into the Gallows House?"

"It was crazy cheap and in a small town where people didn't know about my dad. My mom thinks it's an opportunity to have a real home, like we deserve."

"You *do* deserve a real home," Bailey pointed out as they finally turned onto Willow.

"Well, Tom does, for sure. Fynn's ready to be on his own. He's said it to her enough, but he feels obligated, I think. Like he has to make up for my father leaving by hanging around until my mother gives him her blessing. She likes having us all together, though. She'd have family game night every night if it were up to her."

"And you?" Bailey asked, as they approached the house.

Hunter looked at her, and his face no longer appeared like a mask. She could see the little boy abandoned by his father, the man who had to be strong for his family, the guy she was starting to care for in a way she had never felt.

"I'm starting to like it here, even if I hate the attention the house gets us. There are some nice things in Shadow Springs." He grinned then and her heart leapt.

"You mean me," she said with a toss of her ponytail.

"Humble," he remarked, moving so their bodies were nearly touching.

"That's me," she said, tipping her head back as he dipped his forward.

"*Mijo.*"

His mother's cry forced them apart like a physical push. Bailey's cheeks warmed as the surprisingly short woman rushed forward from the porch.

Hunter's mother was beautiful, with the same sun-kissed skin and dark curls as her son. Her eyes, though large like Hunter's, held that mischievous sparkle that Fynn's did. The overwhelming scent of sage and rosemary enfolded her.

"Hi, Mama. You're home early," Hunter said, accepting a hug.

"I changed my hours at the hotel. I took the night shift so I could make a little more money. Smart, no?" she asked, nudging Bailey.

"Sounds good to me. I'm Bailey, by the way."

She stuck out a hand, which Mrs. Callahan grasped only to pull her forward into an embrace.

"Smart, gracious, and beautiful," she said to Hunter, over Bailey's shoulder. "I approve. Come on in, both of you."

"We have more work to do on the walls," Hunter protested.

"Bailey can help me in the kitchen. First, you both need a snack. I just baked some concha with chocolate." She winked.

"I'm sold." Bailey said.

She wasn't sure what concha was, but was still agreeable to anything with chocolate.

Hunter took her hand and they followed his mother toward the house. Bailey was dizzy with excitement and the sudden change in her relationship with Hunter. It wasn't like they'd actually done anything, aside from holding hands, but in the last few minutes, he'd finally decided to let her in—emotionally and *literally* in... to the Gallows House.

The Gallows House: A West Coast Haunting
by
Sean Tarlove

Pg. 50

After the story of Teresa's murder, the Gallows House remained quiet for several decades, having only two known owners, both of whom were single and relative hermits. In 1969, Basil and Amanda Radcliffe moved in with their teenage daughter, Dorothy, who was also known as Dottie. Dottie was an excellent student and reportedly told anyone who would listen that she planned to study law at Berkley. Amanda was a happy homemaker who also did some dressmaking on the side. Basil had a private practice as a trusted and sought-after obstetrician.

In 1971, during Dottie's senior year, she got engaged to an art student who lived close by, and when she disappeared from high school soon after, it was rumored that she'd run off with her fiancé and started life as a homemaker, forgetting all about her talk of becoming a lawyer.

"It happened all the time," said former Lincoln High School Principal, Ted Daily. "Girls who got engaged so young, they'd drop out. What did they need school for anymore? They used to say they were going to earn their MRS degree."

But Dottie hadn't run off with her fiancé. Instead, she'd suffered the curse of the Gallows House, along with the rest of her family. No one in town knew that Basil had left his practice and stayed inside almost all day and night. They had no idea he had imprisoned his own daughter in the attic, where he tortured her until her death, leaving her to hang there and rot. Why someone like Basil snapped, no one knew, and the truth wasn't discovered until Amanda's body was found tied to the bed in the room they'd shared when a customer came to retrieve a dress she'd ordered and found the door unlocked.

"He barely left the house, they say," Myrtle Smith, the woman who found Mrs. Radcliffe's remains, later recalled. "But he wasn't there the day I showed up. I know it sounds crazy, but I think someone led me to her body. The door was open and I heard someone walking upstairs when I called out. That's why I went in.

I'm not the type to trespass in someone's bedroom. That sick bastard. My guardian angel must've been watching out for me that day. I can only imagine what might have happened had he been there."

Curse? More than one ghost?

Pg. 55

Sheila Nelson moved into the Gallows House after her divorce from her high school sweetheart, in 1988. By this point, the house had quite the reputation, but was affordable for a single teacher like herself.

"Sheila was beautiful and vivacious," said Michelle Sulley, fellow teacher at Lincoln High School. "She loved her students and was known as a kind person. But she did date way too much."

"Sheila often brought her dates home with her," stated Sergeant Quill of the Shadow Springs PD. "Which, normally speaking, is fine. But if you find the wrong guy..."

Was it the wrong guy who imprisoned and raped Sheila in her own home, over a period of several weeks, before finally killing her? Or was it the Gallows House Curse that made Oliver Viceroy do it? Or was it even him? There are a number of people who believe the ghosts in the house are the ones that crave death and torture, and remove the memory of the living that survive.

Plausible? Why leave some alive?

Pg. 60

This brings our story to modern day. The last known owners of the Gallows House were Martin and Eileen Hampstead, who moved in on July 28, 1999. The Hampsteads apparently laughed when they learned the history of the house and the legend it held. Practical and agnostic, they bought the house at a steal, of a price for first-time homeowners, and lived there happily until Martin was fired from his job at an engineering firm in Santa Clarita. From there, things took a downturn. As the readers of this book can probably guess, Martin was found guilty, several months later, of false imprisonment, sexual assault, and first-degree murder.

It is this author's hope that by bringing light to these events, Eileen Hampstead will be the last victim to be claimed by the Gallows House.

Definite pattern. Prolonged torture and murder as the years went on? Or hidden better earlier?

CHAPTER 7

Totally weird how normal everything seemed when she first stepped
foot inside. Bailey didn't know exactly what she'd expected, maybe
a physical difference in the air pressure when she crossed the
threshold, or chains rattling, or... something. But no, it smelled
divine because of sweetcakes surrounded by a cookie crust that
tasted as delicious as they smelled. She even forgave the idea of
being relegated to kitchen duty like it was 1955, assuming she could
pick up some tips from this culinary genius.

"Why has it taken you so long to bring Bailey over?" Mrs.
Callahan chastised as Hunter leaned back in the worn wooden chair,
patting his stomach after his fifth concha.

"Why indeed?" Bailey asked, licking the last bit of sweetness off
her finger.

"Well, she's here now, so you two can be best friends," Hunter
said, pushing away from the table. "I'll get to work on the wall in the
bedroom."

"Relax, it can wait," his mother said. "You have homework, no?"

"Later," he said, though he was already mostly out the kitchen
door.

It was an old house, so no open floor plan, that was for sure. Lots
of smaller-sized rooms with tons of dark wood paneling and creaky
hardwood floors. It was almost like a maze that Mrs. Callahan had
filled with flowering plants and a giant wooden cross in the kitchen.

"Come on then, Bailey. Let's make some enchiladas for dinner.
And if you like it, you can help me prepare for *Dia De Los Muertos*.
It's coming up soon—right after Halloween. I'm planning to make
Pan De Muerto and, if I'm feeling generous, some tamales for
Hunter. They're his favorite."

"Good to know." Bailey stood to join Mrs. Callahan at the sink.
"Thank you for the delicious snack, Mrs. Callahan."

"Call me Estrella," she said with a warm smile and began instructing Bailey on how to put together chicken enchiladas with homemade sauce and pulled chicken left over from the crockpot.

It was so much fun working with Estrella that Bailey almost forgot Hunter was in the house, or what had been pulling her inside for the past year. Eventually though, she decided it was time to ask the friendly woman some questions.

"So how do you like the house?" Bailey asked as she preheated the oven.

"Oh, it's beautiful. So much detail that you don't see in newer homes. Look at the wainscoting and the paneling in the wood," she answered, scooping hand-shredded cheese up to sprinkle on her creation.

"It's really cool," Bailey said, nodding, though she thought it was overkill for a kitchen. Kind of dark and menacing, versus light and airy.

"So, all the rumors are wrong?" Bailey asked. "I mean, about the hauntings?"

Estrella stopped mid-sprinkle, and for the first time the smile faded from her lips. Bailey felt instantly guilty about bringing it up so bluntly.

"I think it's superstition," Estrella said. "But working at hotels, you see and feel things sometimes that you can't always explain, so it's always smart to take precautions."

"Precautions?" Bailey echoed, intrigued.

Estrella's smile returned as she gestured to the giant cross on the wall. "I was raised Catholic," she explained as she put the food in the oven. "I don't really believe so much anymore, but I figure it can't hurt. I also burn sage in the house every afternoon. I read it online. It clears the energy."

Bailey nodded, impressed. "So, if it was haunted, you cleared it out."

"I hope so."

Something in her voice caught, and in Bailey's head it sounded like a siren.

"But?" she prompted.

Estrella sighed, a hand on her hip. "But little things happen that make me wonder. Don't tell the boys, though. I don't want them to worry about what's probably nothing. And I don't care if there is a ghost, it's not chasing me out of my house." Bailey watched Estrella cross herself. For a non-religious woman, she sure was taking a lot of so-called precautions. Before Bailey could ask for more specifics, though, it sounded like something heavy had caused an avalanche above their heads.

"Oh, my god, Hunter," Bailey said as she fled toward the stairs, instantly followed by Estrella.

"I'm okay." Hunter yelled from the top of the steps.

Estrella muttered something in Spanish, and Bailey grabbed the polished banister, pulling herself up the stairs to join Hunter after giving his mom a quick smile.

"What the hell?" she said when she turned the corner and found empty paint cans scattered across the hall.

She turned to the right and found an open doorway, where Hunter sat on his knees, covered in green paint. And he wasn't the only thing covered. Spring Sage coated the newspapers on the floor and part of a step ladder behind him.

"Go back to the kitchen. I got this," Hunter said, not moving.

"Oh, sure. You got it all right," Bailey commented, picking up some of the cans from the hall and setting them right side up in a stack near the doorway. "What happened?"

"I was a klutz," Hunter said, peeling the gloves off his hands. "I guess I left them stacked and they weren't stable. Fynn or somebody must've opened them, that's all. I just didn't think anyone would be stupid enough to pre-open four paint cans. We can't afford this," he spat, throwing the gloves into a puddle of green. "Not money wise or time wise. I'm sick of fixing up this house. I swear I don't think it *wants* to be fixed."

It was more raw emotion than she'd ever seen from Hunter, and Bailey stood silently as he worked the soaked T-shirt off his head. His face and arms were still splattered, along with his too-big jeans. His chest and arms were far more defined than she'd imagined from his lanky body, and Bailey bit her bottom lip to keep her from those kinds of thoughts when he was in the middle of a crisis.

"You think the ghost opened them and knocked them over, don't you?" she asked.

Hunter stared at her, covered in green paint. Green paint with the title of *sage,* which happened to be what Estrella said she used every day on the house to cleanse it.

"No. I think my brother is stupid and careless and wants nothing to do with this house or this family."

Hunter pushed past her, into the hall, and she followed.

"Fynn wants out, okay." Bailey got as far as the bathroom door before he shut it on her. "But I don't think he's malicious or stupid, and I don't think you do either."

The sound of the shower answered her, and Bailey went back to the room to help clean up. By the time Hunter reappeared in the doorway in fresh clothes and wet hair, she'd managed to get everything in decent order. Thankfully, the paint was contained to mostly the tarp and papers he'd put down. But he was right about having to replace the cans.

"Thanks," he said.

"You're welcome." She stood and held out her arms to find herself splotched with green.

"You're welcome to the shower, but all I have are guy clothes," Hunter said and picked up the plaid shirt she'd hung on the doorknob of the room next door.

"Careful. I don't want paint on that."

Hunter held it up and folded it, nodding. "I'll put some clothes on the counter in the bathroom. My mom wants to know if you can stay for dinner."

"She already asked, and I already said yes. My dad works late every night. It's an avoidance issue, and the result is me eating frozen pizza almost daily. So, even if you didn't want me to stay, I'd do it."

Hunter grinned and showed her the bathroom, which she'd already followed him to. When she got out of the shower, she found a pair of Tom's jeans and a white T-shirt she assumed belonged to Fynn, near her own folded plaid shirt. The tee was huge, so she opted for buttoning the plaid shirt instead, being more comfortable swimming in her own brother's clothes. The jeans fit fairly well, disturbingly enough, though they were tight through the hips and loose in the waist. It was good enough for dinner, she reasoned as she finger-combed her hair and left it loose over her shoulders. She didn't wear a lot of makeup anyway, but what she'd had was gone, so the freckles spattered across her nose and cheeks showed up like flashing neon spaceships. Oh well.

"Hunter," she called as she made her way back down the hall.

Heavy footsteps that had to be his answered her from the stairs, so she sighed and headed toward the lower level. He wasn't on the stairs or at the bottom when she reached the banister a few seconds later.

"Hunter?" she asked, more softly.

Maybe he was hiding below, waiting to jump out at her because of her insistence about the ghost.

The moment she set foot on the first step, a wave of heaviness fell over her, making it hard to breathe. Or maybe it was the strange smell in the air, like the cigars her grandpa used to smoke. She shivered and set a hand on the curved railing since it made her a bit dizzy.

Slowly, she crept down, careful because of the weird feeling and the sudden dread that Hunter might actually pop out below. She didn't expect him to be at the top of the stairs since she'd just been there and hadn't seen a sign of him, but heavy footfalls sounded at the top behind her and she jumped. Before she could turn to see him, white mist formed at the bottom of the steps. It swirled into the outline of a woman, reaching out a hand toward Bailey, who stopped short, terrified and in disbelief about what she was seeing.

"*Run*," said a voice in her head.

It was female and echoed like she was in a cave.

Bailey turned to run back up the steps but found black mist swirling there. The dark shadow of a heavy boot reached out from the mist and landed on the second step. A man's laughter filled her head, chasing away the faint echo of the woman's voice still present.

Bailey turned and fled down the stairs toward the white mist that dissipated as she hurtled toward it. She screamed as the footsteps thundered behind her, and two massive hands shoved her from behind, merely a few steps from the bottom. Flying forward, Bailey put her hands up to break her fall. Pain seared through her ankle, but she was barely aware of it because something heavy and smothering landed on top of her, enfolding her entire body in an uncomfortable pressure and that thick smell of tobacco. She tried to roll over, to scream, but she couldn't move. Couldn't breathe.

"Bailey!"

Hunter's voice broke through the fog and she was free, like it had never happened. Except it *had* and her ankle smarted to prove it as he knelt beside her and gathered her into his lap.

Hysterical sobbing wasn't something Bailey enjoyed, but she couldn't help it. The smothering sensation and the malice that exuded from the black mist and whatever was on top of her—whatever had pushed her down the stairs—it was burned in her memory and she couldn't make sense of it.

"It's okay," Hunter said, rocking her awkwardly.

Estrella ran in and out with ice packs and bandages, and eventually Bailey calmed down.

"Did you fall?" Estrella asked, worrying at a small silver cross on her breast.

Bailey shook her head.

"The jeans I gave you were too long?" Hunter guessed. "They tripped you, didn't they?"

"I was pushed," Bailey said, standing and wincing when she put weight on her ankle.

Estrella crossed herself again and Hunter half-laughed, like he thought maybe he was supposed to take it as a joke.

"It still hurts where he shoved me," Bailey said, turning and looking over her shoulder. She hadn't realized it at first because of the shock and the pain in her ankle. It felt like someone had scraped the skin on her back. Hunter reached for her and she shied away when he brushed the spot. Carefully, he picked up the bottom of the shirt and lifted it to reveal her bra strap and bare back. Judging from the intake of breath from both Estrella and Hunter, something was there.

"What? What is it?" she asked, starting to panic.

Hunter pulled out his phone and snapped a pic before handing it to her and letting her shirt fall back over her. Bailey stared. It was like everything stopped and the house began to spin. Ten angry red scratches in the shape and spread of two hands covered her skin.

"I have to go," Bailey choked out and ran through the front door, injured ankle and all.

She couldn't process what was happening, especially with Estrella and Hunter's worried faces hovering above her.

Bailey made it home in under two minutes and fought with the key in the door until it let her inside. She shot straight up the stairs and into Caleb's room, where she stripped off her clothes and pulled on a fresh plaid shirt before climbing into the bed with the rest. Tears leaked from the corners of her eyes, but she ignored them, as they were nothing compared to the emotional release she'd had earlier in front of Hunter. What she needed to do was record everything that happened and add it to the corkboard. She knew she should do it while it was fresh in her mind, but she couldn't make herself move from the fetal position on her dead brother's bed.

What was that thing? And what or who was the *other* thing? What did the white and black mists mean? Was the woman trying to warn her? It sure seemed like it, and she was stupid enough to be too scared to listen. More than anything, she was ashamed of her base reaction now that something had finally happened to her—and inside the Gallows House.

If she was lucky enough to be given a second encounter, she promised herself she'd suck it up and stay calm.

CHAPTER 8

Twenty minutes later the doorbell rang. Bailey debated staying in bed, but the incessant knocking that followed forced her out and down the stairs, groaning. She pulled on her sweatpants as she went.

The moment she opened the door, Hunter walked past her with two plates full of delicious smelling food. He headed straight for the kitchen table, which was covered in old piles of mail yet to be gone through. After shoving it over to make space, he placed the food down and held out a chair for her.

Her grumbling stomach won out and she joined him, despite the delicious pastry she'd devoured a mere hour earlier. It helped that he sat and started eating, not really paying extra attention to her or asking a million worried questions, like her father would have if he were home.

Estrella's food tasted incredible, and they downed the whole thing in silence, Bailey rising only to retrieve a couple sodas from the fridge to wash it down. When they'd finished, she leaned back in her chair and watched Hunter rinse the dishes in the sink, his shoulders and head hunched over them. He always gave his utmost attention to whatever he was doing at the moment. *That's why his eyes always feel so intense.* When he listened to her, it was like there was nothing or no one else in the world. She was the center of his universe, even if only for the two minutes it took to discuss homework.

"Thank you," she said as he dried his hands on an old kitchen towel.

"I heard you're the one who helped make it. I figured it wouldn't be fair if you didn't get to eat it, too."

"I mean, for being so cool about… well, everything."

"That's me, Mr. Cool."

Bailey couldn't help but laugh at the ridiculous move he made, crisscrossing his arms with a dip of his knees.

"How's your back?" he asked, squatting down beside her so they were at eye level.

"I don't feel any pain anymore. I'm afraid to look, though."

"I'll look if you want," he said softly.

Bailey turned and moved her now-dry hair forward over her shoulder. Hunter's warm breath tickled the back of her neck and a chill of excitement traveled down her spine. He was so close. Gently, he gripped the bottom of the flannel she had on and lifted, letting his fingers brush the bare skin of her back. She realized she wasn't wearing a bra, because she had stripped everything off when she'd gotten home. Her cheeks flushed, but she didn't move as the pads of his fingers ran over the spot on her back that had hurt so much—and so recently. Now she felt only electric tingles of excitement from his touch.

"It's gone," Hunter said, letting her shirt fall back in place.

Bailey turned back to face him. He was so close, centimeters from her. Their breath mingled in the air and his scent of home-baked love that made so much more sense now, filled her with comfort.

"I shouldn't have left like that. I'm sorry." She got caught in his eyes.

"I don't blame you. I didn't think it would bother you or do something like that. I'm the one who's sorry." Hunter took her hands in his without breaking eye contact.

He lightly stroked her knuckles with his thumbs and the electric shivers returned.

"Wait," she said, pulling back and breaking the spell. "You didn't think it would? Does that mean you knew there was something in your house?"

Hunter collapsed back, cross-legged on the kitchen tile, and blew out a heavy breath like he was a deflating balloon.

"Yes. I knew there was something in the house the minute we moved in. It was never more than a feeling or a quick movement out of the corner of my eye. Footsteps in the hall. That sort of thing. And Mama was so happy, so committed to making this a happily ever after, finally after all she'd—we'd—been through. So I pretended not to notice. I figured I'm a big guy and could handle it."

"But I'm just a little girl."

Anger heated her neck and face. He didn't say it, but if the entity had attacked *her* specifically, wasn't that what it was thinking, too?

"You're a tough woman," Hunter corrected, and put his palms up in surrender.

"Apparently not. I ran scared. But it won't happen again. Why didn't you tell me, though?"

Hunter shrugged. "I guess I figured you were curious like everyone else in this town. I want them to leave us alone, and a couple footsteps and moving shadows doesn't mean I want my home turned into a zoo."

"You thought that's what I'd do?" Bailey asked, standing.

It hurt to hear him say it. And maybe he wasn't far off about her having ulterior motives, but not that.

"No—I mean, I didn't know," Hunter said, standing also. "Look, I didn't know you that well yet. I let you in today, didn't I? It's because I trust you, Bailey. And I don't trust a lot of people."

Bailey's temper instantly cooled. She thought about what he'd said earlier, about his father and how they'd moved all over, their debt. But he'd glossed over what was probably the worst part. He'd mentioned how he wanted to be where no one knew them or his dad. That meant when people did, they treated him like trash. Probably like he was a felon, too.

"I'm glad you trust me," Bailey said, closing the distance between them, standing on tiptoe and kissing his cheek. "I won't let you down."

"And I won't let you get hurt," he said, taking her face into his hands.

"You're not banning me from the house," Bailey warned as he stroked her cheeks with his thumbs.

"Then I'm not leaving you alone for a second when you're over."

Maybe she could handle that.

The next thing Bailey knew, Hunter's lips were on hers, soft yet insistent. She parted her own, letting him know she wanted this, and the kiss lingered as he explored her mouth, tentatively at first, and then with more abandon. Bailey threw her arms around his neck and tangled her fingers in his thick curls, trying to pull him closer. Every inch of her was alive with desire and she suddenly knew what it meant to lose herself in someone else.

After a few minutes, Hunter let his hands fall to her waist, where he literally swept her off her feet so they were level. They made-out for a while before finally parting, lips swollen and raw, faces flushed.

"I want to show you something," Bailey said, taking his hand and leading him toward the stairs.

"I don't have any protection—"

She flashed him a look. "That's *not* what I was going to show you."

He gave her a sheepish smile and then followed, this time silently.

When Hunter stepped inside Caleb's room, he took it all in, not moving as Bailey shut the door behind him. She motioned for him to sit on the corner of the bed and he did so, waiting patiently.

"This," Bailey said, pulling out the corkboard from beneath the desk, "is something I haven't shared with anyone. Not even Charity."

She set it on the bed beside him and let him examine it, his bushy brows furrowed in concentration as he scanned each scrap of paper or picture.

"I don't understand." He rested a finger on the picture of the Gallows House, his house.

"He was obsessed."

Bailey had never said that out loud. Yes, Charity knew she suspected there were clues there, but not the extent of her own obsession.

"My brother. He did the same report we're working on, and from what I can tell, that's when he started going a little too overboard. I found this," she said, pulling out the worn book from the nightstand and holding it out to him.

Hunter thumbed through it, pausing at the pages with the most highlighter or hand-written notes jammed in the margins.

"And you think the house had something to do with his death?" He searched her eyes.

"I'm certain of it," Bailey said, trembling because she'd put it all out there on the line to be seen and judged by someone other than herself. "There's more. See here?" She pointed to the portion of the board that had the lines connecting Amber's picture and the house.

"They were the closest couple at school until they went in the house together. He found a way inside, on January third, I think."

"The day he died," Hunter said, looking at the obituary, also on the board.

"Yes, earlier. He and Amber went, but whatever happened there—and something *did*—made her leave. And I mean town, not only Caleb. When we tried to contact her about his funeral, she accused him of horrible things."

Bailey swallowed back the thickness building in her throat. Tears had begun to gather behind her eyes and she was finding it harder and harder to talk. But now that she'd started, she had to finish. She had to get it all out. She was unravelling almost a year of pain and suspicion and it felt right.

"Things I know he would *never* do or try to do," she clarified, unable to say the words. "And what kind of girlfriend, who supposedly loved someone, would up and run away early to college and not come back when she found out her boyfriend had died?"

Bailey heard her voice grow high and panicked. She felt the tears begin to burst through and trickle down her cheeks, but she kept going.

"I'm telling you, I don't know what happened that night, but whatever it was killed Caleb."

When she finished, she collapsed onto the bed next to Hunter, unable to look at him.

Silence.

"I see," Hunter said, minutes later.

That was it? He saw? What did that mean?

"So this whole time you've been trying to get me to invite you inside my house so you could search for clues about your brother's death." It was a statement, cold and accusatory, and Bailey's heart about tore in two.

"I'm sorry. It was before I knew you. I couldn't just tell you what I thought. You would've said I was crazy."

She was sorry if it hurt him at all, but she wasn't sorry she'd done it. It was her life's purpose, and nothing—not even a guy—was going to change that.

"It wasn't only before you knew me, though," Hunter said, clenching some of the blankets in his fists. "It's why you accepted my mother's invitation today. It's why you were in my house. It's why you said you won't stay away, and it's probably why that thing attacked you."

Bailey sat stunned, tears falling freely and mouth hanging open.

He was right, so there wasn't much she could say in her defense. But really? Couldn't he see what this meant? How could Hunter, of all people, make this about him?

"So," Hunter said, standing when she didn't answer. "The thing in my house with my family, my mother and little brother, is dangerous." He rubbed both hands down over his face.

"Well, I would think that was obvious after what happened to me today."

Hunter looked at her, face twisted in some kind of pain. "I'm sorry about Caleb, Bailey. I really am. I can't imagine losing my brother." He stepped forward and grasped her arms. "But don't you see that if you'd told me sooner, you could've prevented something else bad from happening?"

"Nothing else did happen," Bailey spat. "If that would've made a difference, then you wouldn't have bought the house after finding out so many people died in it. Why is my brother any different?"

"Because he's your brother," Hunter said, in his quiet voice, letting go of her.

Bailey stood staring at the boy she'd been making-out with less than an hour ago like he was a million miles away. She thought if she shared her burden, she'd feel lighter. That she'd have a kindred spirit, someone to move forward with. Instead, it had wedged a wall between them. That's what she got for sharing her feelings. For letting in someone else who could turn around and hurt her. Desert her.

"I should probably go before your dad gets home and finds me up here."

Bailey didn't trust her words anymore, so she simply nodded, looking away and out the window in silent dismissal. She heard the door creak open, and seconds later the front door shut. And just like that, he was gone. What was she supposed to do now? The next day was the Friday before Halloween. Was she supposed to act like nothing had happened between them?

Bailey grabbed the corkboard and shoved it back under the desk, but try as she might, she couldn't find the book she'd shown Hunter. Had he taken it with him to read more about the house?

She pulled out her phone to text him, then stopped. What was so wrong if he did? Wasn't it a good idea for him to learn as much as possible about his own house? And was she being selfish? It was where he and his family lived. What would it feel like if she couldn't sleep safely in her own home?

Head aching and exhausted from the emotional rollercoaster that day, Bailey shut the door on Caleb's room and went back to her own, where she climbed in bed and flipped off the lights, despite it being only eight o'clock.

As she began to doze off, her phone buzzed. She rubbed her tired eyes and focused on the short text that had come in from Charity. Three numbers that washed all the fatigue from her body and put her on high alert.

911.

CHAPTER 9

"What happened?" Bailey asked the moment Charity picked up.

"Fynn was put in the back of a police car," came the high-pitched reply. "I can't get ahold of Hunter. He's not answering my texts."

"What'd he do?" Bailey met Charity's panic with her own. When she'd left Fynn, he was with Tom at Molly's, flirting with Sam.

"I don't know exactly. I think maybe he was harassing someone. He was acting like he was drunk or high. He kept swearing at the officer that handcuffed him. This is horrible. What do we do?"

"I'll get Hunter. Where are you?"

"At the corner by the school, across from my aunt's. The house with the inflatable dragon that breathes fire."

Bailey hung up. Only in Shadow Springs could you identify landmarks based on Halloween decorations. She pulled on a pair of checkered high-tops and rushed out the door, dialing Hunter on repeat. It was when she got to the walkway at the Gallows House that she heard the click meaning he'd finally picked up.

Bailey nearly collapsed with relief and started talking immediately.

"Where have you been? Did you get Charity's texts? It's Fynn, he's been arrested."

"Oh, no," said a voice, way too deep to be Hunter's. Then laughter.

The same male laughter she'd heard when she was pushed down the stairs. Bailey dropped the phone to her side and ran for the door. Could ghosts get inside phones? Or did it have Hunter's? She couldn't go any further with that line of thought. She *had* to get inside.

She raised a hand to pound on the door, but it opened to let her in, like the house had been expecting her. Trying not to think about it, she rushed inside and started calling Hunter's name as the door shut behind her.

Seconds later, Hunter flew down the stairs, four at a time.

"Bailey. What is it? What's wrong?" He grabbed her by the arms again, but this time to try and ground her.

"Where's your phone?"

Hunter frowned and glanced back at the stairs. "It's in my room, where I was 'til you came in here screaming. Why?"

"Charity and I have been calling and texting you and you wouldn't answer. It's about Fynn. He's in the back of a police car. We have to go. Now."

She watched as the information clicked in his head, and followed as he rushed out the door, searching both directions like a lost child.

"This way," she said, taking his hand and running.

She got him there in under five minutes, with a stitch in her side and chest in pain. Three police cars sat in or half-on the driveway, and the dragon lay deflated on the grass, the fog machine spraying out a low mist that swallowed their feet below the shins.

Charity rushed up to meet them and pointed to the car in the driveway, with blue and red flashing silently, coloring the eerie fog with a dizzying light show. She gripped Bailey's arm so tight it hurt, but Bailey merely watched, catching her breath while Hunter rushed toward the car.

They watched as he spoke animatedly with the officer, who stood outside the open backdoor, hovering protectively. When the officer motioned for Hunter to follow him to the house, Bailey caught a glimpse of Fynn seated inside the back of the patrol car, head leaned back against the leather, one leg outstretched and dangling outside the car. His perfect hair was messed up and his shirt was open to the navel and untucked, revealing a muscular chest with scratch marks down the front.

Bailey gasped. It looked like the picture of what had happened to her earlier. Without thinking, she jogged over to Fynn and rested a hand on the top of the open door, leaning in.

"Fynn," she whispered.

His head lolled to the side, facing her, and his eyes popped open, black orbs reflecting the colors of the siren. Bailey repressed a shudder.

"Are you okay?" she asked. "What happened?"

For a split second, she thought he grinned in an unnatural way, but as quickly as the flash of red from the overhead lights changed to blue, the image was gone.

"I don't remember," Fynn said, shutting his eyes again.

"Come on, Fynn. Seriously. Did something attack you?" Bailey poked at the scratches on his chest.

He shrugged. Bailey stepped back, frustrated, in time to see Hunter approach with the officer again.

"Step away from the suspect, please, miss." The officer's hand rested on the top of the weapon at his hip.

The sight of the gun, even holstered, made Bailey want to hyperventilate. She backed away, obliging.

"What's he suspected of?" she asked, focusing on Hunter's blank face.

His body language said a lot more than his poker face, that was for sure. Every muscle was taut. She could've plucked any tendon in his body like a guitar string.

"Who are you, miss?" the officer asked, sounding tired.

"A friend of the family," Hunter answered, pulling her aside and down the drive, away from the dizzying lights and damp mist.

"Did you see the scratches?" Bailey asked, as Hunter backed them farther and farther away, to where Charity waited, chewing on her lip.

"Yeah. They were from Sam. Apparently, he got the wrong message from her and she had to fend him off."

"*What*?" Bailey said, incredulous.

She was the one all over him earlier. He couldn't have cared less.

Hunter pulled a hand back through his own mussed hair, like he was searching for his baseball cap.

"Apparently they'd been drinking, and when she rebuffed his advances, he lost it. He went at her and she scratched him, so he turned his attack to the inflatable in the yard. He slayed the dragon," he added sarcastically.

"Yikes," Charity said, staring at the carnage on the lawn.

"She says she won't press charges if he pays for the decoration," Hunter finished, lowering his head.

"That seems reasonable," Charity said.

Bailey was silent.

"They want three hundred dollars." Hunter kicked at some loose pebbles on the road. "Between that and the paint cans from earlier, that's a huge expense for us."

And now everyone would be talking about his brother, thought Bailey. Maybe not like his dad, but close enough to hit a sore spot.

Bailey reached for his hand, but he pulled it away and stuffed it in his pocket.

"Should we call your mom?" she asked. "And what about Tom? Where is he?"

"She's asleep," Hunter said, sharply. "And if we can keep them from pressing charges, then I don't see why we need to worry her. I don't know where Tomas went. Shit."

"I'll ask the officer if he knows," Bailey volunteered and jogged back over without waiting for a response.

"Excuse me, sir?" Bailey asked a different officer, who seemed slightly more approachable.

The older guy looked familiar. It was possible he'd been part of the investigation into Caleb's death.

"Yes?" He smiled.

"Um, I was wondering if there was a young boy here at all? Tomas Callahan? He's the, um, accused's brother."

The man excused himself and Bailey waited as he spoke with another officer, then returned with a smile and tip of his cap.

"The young lady involved reported that he'd left the ice cream parlor with friends, earlier this evening."

"Thank you," she said, relieved.

"Sergeant Harper. If you need anything, Miss Thompson."

So, he did know her.

Bailey nodded and went back to report to the others, where Hunter held up his hands, helplessly.

"I don't have my phone, and I guess it's not working right, anyway, since I didn't get your messages. How am I supposed to get ahold of him? He better be home by curfew."

"He will," Bailey assured him, finding it really hard not to touch him in a reassuring way. It was clearly not something he wanted right now. "He's a good kid."

Hunter nodded, Adam's apple bobbing like a lump stuck in his throat.

"I can run back and grab your phone," Bailey offered.

Hunter shot her a look that made her jump.

"No. Thank you. Not without me."

"What is going on with you two?" Charity stepped between them. "The tension is hotter than dragon's breath. Well, working dragon's breath."

"Nothing," they both answered simultaneously.

"Whatever." Charity shook Bailey's shoulders like she could rattle sense into her. "But someone needs to go back and get it, and someone needs to stay here and find out if they're dropping the charges."

Bailey looked at Hunter, waiting for his decision.

"Bailey, he likes you. Try to convince him to agree to apologize and pay for the stupid dragon. I'll get my phone. It won't take long."

Bailey nodded and watched him run off down the street. Then, ignoring Charity's questions about what was going on, she approached the car where Harper and the other officer stood.

"Sergeant Harper, may I speak to Fynn, please? I think I may be able to convince him to apologize."

"Be my guest," he said, backing away from the door.

When the other officer tried to protest, Sergeant Harper, who she guessed was his senior, glared until he quieted down and moved away to give her some privacy.

"Hey, Fynn," Bailey said, trying to get him to open his eyes again.

"Hmm?" He didn't oblige.

"It's me. Bailey. Listen, you want to get out of those handcuffs, right?"

He raised his cuffed hands and motioned for her to come closer. Bailey shifted and checked to see that the cops weren't far away, then leaned in low where the carbon dioxide from the fog machine hit her nose and gave her a damp chill.

Fynn leaned toward her, and his alcohol-smelling breath moved the tiny hairs surrounding her ear.

"Depends," he whispered. "I want 'em off if I'm going to jail. I'll keep 'em on if you're taking me home."

Bailey froze, stunned. Sure, he'd been flirtatious, and yes, he was probably only a couple years older, but still. She'd never had anyone say something like that to her, especially someone close to someone she cared about, and she didn't know what to do, so she continued on as if he'd never said it.

"Well, if you don't want to go to jail, you need to say you're sorry to Sam and agree to pay for the dragon you busted."

Fynn snapped his head up, and his eyes opened so fast Bailey nearly hit her head on the car in her rush to back up.

"She's the one who should apologize to me. *Bitch*. Did you see what she did to my chest?" He pulled at the loose-hanging shirt and showed off the scratches and sculpted muscles.

"Calm down or they really will take you away to jail," she hissed, making excuses in her head about it being the alcohol talking. "Even if you don't mean it, say you're sorry. It's not that hard."

"Would you say something you didn't mean to take away the pain, Bailey?" he asked, sounding suddenly completely sober while looking her straight in the eyes.

Was it the red lights of the police car reflecting there?

"I guess so, yeah. In this case, it's the right thing to do. For Hunter and Tom's sake. For your mom."

"I'm not interested in them, Bailey. I'm interested in you." He was back to being drunk and obnoxious. "I'll tell you what. I'll say I'm sorry if you say please."

"Please." Bailey was so angry at this asshole that she could punch him.

"Nah. That was too easy." He leaned out the side of the car, making her trot backward a couple of steps. "I'll say sorry if you agree to go out with me."

Bailey froze once again. He wasn't serious. That was worse than his crack about the handcuffs.

"I can't," she croaked, looking around to see who might be listening.

Other than Charity watching from the foot of the driveway, no one was.

"You're too old."

"I'm twenty. You're what—seventeen?" he asked, holding the car door with both hands to try and pry himself to standing.

She didn't answer. Because if she were truthful, she was turning eighteen in less than a month. That made it all seem less far-fetched.

Still, she couldn't date him. He was being an asshole. Plus, she kissed his brother.

Fynn succeeded in getting to a standing position outside the police car, and stumbled toward her. Bailey fought not to run. That would be ridiculous. The police were steps away. This was the same guy she sat next to only hours ago at Molly's and in his truck.

"Please just say you're sorry." Her voice was shaking, which made her mad at herself. "Then we can all go home."

"I like the way you sound when you say please," he said, too close to her now.

Bailey planted her feet in the ground beneath the mist, and gathered her wits about her. He was infuriating and rude, but she'd survived being pushed down the stairs by a ghost earlier.

"Tell you what, say you're sorry and that you'll replace the dragon, and when you're sober again, ask me out and we'll talk about it."

"Fine. I'm tired of this shit anyway. These would be far more fun on you." Fynn lifted his handcuffed hands as Hunter stepped up beside her.

Bailey relaxed, leaning toward the comfort of his body, whether he was mad at her or not.

Fynn took three big steps forward, pushing between her and Hunter, and paused to look at her.

"But you know I'm sexier than Hunter, and I know how to make you say please."

Before Bailey could react, Hunter had shoved his brother to the ground and was pounding a fist into his face. Charity screamed and the police seemed to take way too long to drag him off.

Bailey shook her head, speechless as Hunter pulled away from Sergeant Harper's grasp and shoved his hair back off his forehead. He crossed his fingers above his head as he glared at Fynn, who was being helped to his feet by the other officer.

"I won't press charges, officers. He's just jealous of his better-looking brother," Fynn said. "Now where's Samantha? I'm ready to apologize so I can get the hell out of this shithole."

CHAPTER 10

Bailey didn't sleep well. She'd made it home just before her dad, but she was plagued by dreams of the deep voice laughing at her and locking her in small spaces—and that was especially strange, considering she wasn't normally claustrophobic. She woke late, and by the time she got to Hunter's house, he was gone. So, either he didn't wait for her that day, or waited and gave up.

"You look terrible," Charity said, when they finally saw each other in History, but she was talking to Hunter.

If Bailey had a rough night, by the looks of it Hunter's was way worse. Dark circles rimmed his eyes like shallow graves, making his normally warm, chocolate-chip eyes appear sunken and void-like. His skin was sallow and the golden-brown hue that made her think of sunshine was tinged with a sickly shade of green, like he might run out of the room to vomit at any moment.

"Seriously," Leah chimed in, and Bailey wished she could banish her somewhere—at least temporarily—while they discussed what'd happened. "We're still on for tomorrow night, though, right? I'm so psyched about getting to go in the Gallows House on Halloween."

Bailey watched Hunter grip his pencil tighter as he spun it in his hands. The tips of his fingers turned white.

"About that," Bailey said. "We found a copy of that book Charity saw on the Internet, and between that and Hunter's pics, I don't think it'll be necessary."

Hunter stopped spinning the pencil and glanced at her, mouth open in surprise. He wasn't the only one. Charity nearly fell out of her chair and had to grasp the edges of her desk to keep from making a scene. Bailey ignored her.

"Who made you the group leader?" Leah asked.

"She's right," Hunter said. "It's not necessary, and things are going to be busy at my place. My mom is preparing for the Day of the Dead celebration, and my little brother will probably want to go trick-or-treating."

Leah bristled, but pasted on a saccharine smile for Hunter's sake. "So where is this book?"

"Bailey has it," Hunter said.

"Actually, I believe you do." Bailey forced a grin. "Things were a little crazy. You took it with you, remember?"

Hunter appeared fully awake and aware now, and narrowed his eyes enough to send Bailey a signal. He obviously had no idea what she was talking about.

"Well, anyway," Bailey said, "it's somewhere, so we'll find it. The rough draft isn't due 'til Wednesday, so it'll be fine."

It had to still be in Caleb's room somewhere. She'd just missed it because she was upset.

"You can't offer up the invitation of the year and then renege." Leah pouted her full lips. "I told people I was going. I bought a Ouija board."

"No Ouija," both Bailey and Hunter said at once.

Leah rolled her eyes. "If you think no one else has done that over the years, you're insane. There are probably a hundred accounts online of people contacting spirits on the grounds alone. Hell, we've all heard the story about Ashley's brother's friend who said the planchet flew off the board, hovered, then hit him in the head."

"Why would you want that?" Charity asked, and Bailey felt a swell of appreciation for her friend.

Leah shrugged. "It's Halloween and it's fun."

The bell rang and they all trudged toward the exit, with Leah continuing to try different tactics, from flirtatious to angry, to get Hunter to let her come over. Bailey was about to blow her cool, when Fynn's familiar red pickup pulled in front of the steps, blocking their path and attracting a lot of whispers and attention.

Fynn threw it into park and leaned out the passenger side, looking like his usual every-hair-in-place self.

"I'm here to apologize," he announced.

It was Leah who stepped forward with a devilish look and a toss of her hair.

"You must be the older brother," she cooed.

"That's me," he agreed, holding out a hand. "Fynn Callahan, at your service."

"Leah Tucker."

Fynn pressed his lips to the back of her hand and winked before leaning over toward the others.

"Bailey, Hunter was supposed to tell you, but judging by the look on your face, he hasn't. It doesn't matter, though. I need to apologize in person, so here I am."

Bailey felt Hunter at her back and knew he must be horrified by all the attention.

"Can we not do this right now?" She hugged her books to her chest.

"Just say you forgive me. I honestly didn't remember any of it until Hunter started wailing on me. But he's filled me in and I'm ashamed of myself."

"Fine. I forgive you," Bailey said, moving away from the truck.

"Let's try again, please?" he asked, sounding earnest and ashamed. "Molly's? My treat? Then I can at least explain what happened as far as I know."

"I was there, and I wasn't drunk," Bailey hissed at him so only the people closest could hear. "I don't need to know what happened."

"She forgave you, bro," Hunter said, stepping up beside Bailey and taking her arm.

She hadn't realized until that moment that she'd been trembling, and she didn't know if it was anger or stress or fear.

She let Hunter guide her around the front of the truck and away toward Willow. Surprisingly, no one followed them, and once they'd turned onto the quiet of the lonely street Bailey relaxed a little.

"Thank you," Hunter said, before she could do the same.

She gaped at him.

"For stepping in about Halloween and for being so cool about what happened with Fynn." Hunter winced like he thought she might slap him and run.

"You're welcome," Bailey said, unsure what to do.

"And I hope that if you can forgive my brother, you'll forgive me, too. For leaving yesterday."

A part of her wanted to jump into his arms and start kissing him right there. Another part wanted to argue more about how he'd grown cold at the mention of her brother and finding evidence in the house. Still, a third part wanted to run home and hide in Caleb's bed and try to get some actual sleep.

Hunter solved her dilemma by offering his hand to her, which she took as they strolled down the path.

"Fynn says he really doesn't remember anything," Hunter started.

"I believe it," Bailey said. "He was drunk off his ass."

"That's the thing, though." Hunter squeezed her hand a little tighter. "He doesn't drink. Neither of us do. We swore off any substance use when our dad went to prison. He had a blood alcohol content of three times the legal limit when he shot that policeman."

Bailey tried to swallow the information down, along with the lump in her throat.

"Maybe he'll remember why he doesn't do it, and it won't happen again," she said, not at all confident in her words.

"I just don't understand why he did it in the first place. And that's the weird thing."

Hunter stopped walking and pulled Bailey under the cover of a weeping willow on the neighboring lawn. It wasn't the ancient giant on the Gallows lawn, but it was beautiful. The long wispy leaves curtained them in an illusion of privacy, though no one else was ever on the street at this time of the day.

Bailey waited for him to continue as he worked through something in his head.

"He says he doesn't even remember taking the first drink, or anything after he and Sam left Molly's when her shift was over."

"Maybe he's embarrassed?"

Hunter frowned. "No. You should've seen how upset he was. He actually cried, Bailey. Real tears. And I've never seen him do that, not even when our dad left."

Bailey fell silent, working it out in her head. She recalled the horrible things Fynn had said and done, which clashed with the charming, albeit flirtatious, version of Fynn she'd known before.

"Remember what you told me about your brother?" Hunter whispered like he might be overheard. "How you know him and how he'd never do those things he was accused of? Or take his life? I get it now. I… I know Fynn and Caleb were probably very different people, and I'm not trying to compare them, but the feeling is the same."

Bailey's chest grew tight with the pain of the memories and the pain on Hunter's face. She cared about Hunter. Really cared. She'd let him in, and it wasn't only because she liked kissing him. He was a good guy, honest and caring, especially when it came to his family. But he'd already threatened to leave her behind, once.

"So, you think that whatever happened to Caleb may be happening to Fynn?"

"I don't know what I think exactly. But I was wondering." he shifted from one foot to another before forcing himself to look straight at her. "If we work together, maybe we can figure it out and drive out whatever's doing this."

Bailey's breath caught in her throat. This was what she'd wanted when she'd bared her soul to him yesterday. She had no words, so she simply nodded and squeezed his hand.

A weight seemed to physically lift off Hunter's shoulders and he stood taller and more relaxed, gifting her with one of his rare unfiltered smiles.

"I couldn't sleep last night, so I did some online research," he said with a burst of renewed energy.

Bailey wished she had done the same instead of trying to fight through her dreams.

"Ghosts feed off energy, so when people start to notice them and react, they get stronger. That's why hauntings usually start out small and escalate."

They reached the Gallows House, and instead of inviting her in, Hunter kept hold of her hand and continued talking animatedly as he pulled her into the house.

"It seems like it's more likely to be a ghost than a demon since there were plenty of people that died violently here."

A thump in the kitchen made Bailey jump.

"Is your mom home?"

Hunter shook his head, furrowing his brow and keeping firm hold of her hand. Together, they crept toward the sound and hesitated only a moment before bursting into the kitchen. At first, Bailey saw nothing amiss. But the moment she started to let out the breath she'd been holding, every cupboard door slowly swung open in front of their eyes. The drawers began to rattle as Hunter squeezed her hand tighter and took a tentative step toward the island in the center, where a coffee mug slid about six inches toward him.

Bailey released his hand and tried to remind herself of her pledge not to run again if she were lucky enough to encounter something in this house. That was easier said than done, though, when Hunter reached for the handle of the now-still mug and all hell broke loose. The rattling drawers flew open one after another as the cupboard doors began to slam over and over again. Utensils flew, scattering over the tile floor and stone countertops. The mug, now forgotten centimeters from Hunter's hand, crashed to the floor at his feet, making Bailey scream. The cacophony surrounding them seemed to react in kind, kicking up the chaos of scraping kitchen tools, shattering dishes, and banging cabinets.

"Come on," Hunter hissed, tugging her hand away from her ears as the refrigerator opened itself and began tossing out its contents like a toddler having a tantrum.

Bailey stood still, unsure if retreating was the right thing to do, until every sharp object in the butcher block on the counter unsheathed with a screech. A steak knife sailed past Bailey's shoulder and embedded itself in the wall behind her, close enough to feel the breeze rush by her ear. Hunter yanked her hand hard, pulling her out of shock and into action. Together, they bolted toward the back door as a butcher knife struck the center. The two ducked behind the island and Hunter reached up to open the door but found it locked.

"What do we do?" Bailey half-shouted, half-cried, as he battled with the doorknob, to no avail.

Ominous male laughter echoed all around, mocking them. Bailey watched as the cross on the wall began to spin. Hunter braced himself, breathing heavily in what appeared to be anger as he peered above the counter, and a pot flew past and clattered to the ground beside Bailey.

After grabbing the handle, Bailey led Hunter to the other side of the island. It seemed silly, since she knew whatever was in the room could see it all, but at least it offered a bit of a shield. When they reached the entrance, where the shards of the coffee cup littered the floor, Bailey grabbed Hunter's hand and pulled him back as a platter flew, frisbee-like, where his head would've been. They stared at each other, wide-eyed, and somehow it gave her the strength to get her wits about her.

She counted silently to three and jumped up, holding the pan like a baseball bat. She wasn't the best at sports, but she'd played some softball in her day, and when the next object came shooting at her, she swung, sending it across the room to shatter on the opposite side of the island. Hunter grabbed her shoulder and they both ran out of the room and right through the front door, not stopping until they were below the willow where Beckham had hung himself over a century earlier.

"Are you okay?" Hunter breathed, holding her at arm's length, making sure she was unharmed.

"Fine," Bailey assured him. "But I don't think it likes me very much."

Hunter pulled her close and held her to him. She rested her head against his chest, his heartbeat thudding against her ear in a hurried rhythm.

"Maybe it's angry that you were researching it," she said, when he finally loosened his grip.

"Then why didn't it do something to the computer last night? It obviously could have. When I finally got my phone last night, the battery was completely drained, and I know it had at least a sixty percent charge when I set it down."

"Why would it hate me?" Bailey asked, hoping she didn't sound as freaked out as she felt.

"I don't know, but we'll figure it out," Hunter assured her. "And until then, I think you really should stay out of there."

Grudgingly, Bailey followed Hunter to her house. She couldn't help wonder if it was trying to keep her out of the house because it knew she could find something important.

Glancing back one last time, she was sure she saw a human-shaped shadow standing in the attic window, watching.

CHAPTER 11

The door was unlocked when they got to the house, and Bailey's dad looked as shocked to see them as they were to see him. He still had his work clothes on and he was sitting on the couch, looking at what Bailey soon realized were photos of Caleb when he was a baby.

"You're home early," Bailey said, with as much positivity as she could muster.

She knew her dad would never let her upstairs alone with a boy, which was beyond stupid since she could normally do whatever she wanted. And right then, what she really wanted was to work in Caleb's room with Hunter.

"I thought I'd surprise you and we could have a movie night." Her dad set the pictures aside gingerly and stood, offering a hand to Hunter. "I'm Gerald Thompson."

"Hunter Callahan," he said, shaking his hand while shifting awkwardly on his feet.

"Hunter and I were going to work on our report that's due early in the week."

"Oh. Well, I'm sure if it's waited this long, it can wait another day or so. I downloaded some horror films and I have a bag of kettle corn. I even have cider heating in the crockpot. That was always your favorite. And I've made a new batch of cookies."

Her dad seemed so hopeful, almost like a little boy. But why did he have to pick *then* to have a breakthrough moment?

"It's okay," Hunter said. "You should spend time with your dad. We can meet tomorrow. Maybe work while we hand out candy to trick-or-treaters. We can set up on the walkway in front of my house. I should probably spend some time with my own family, anyway."

Bailey understood. He was worried about leaving his family alone in that house. At the same time, she was just as worried about him. She wished they could move out until they were able to figure things out.

Hunter saw her hesitation and let his fingers brush against hers, sending an unexpected tingle up her arm. She smiled and nodded.

"Okay, Dad. But I have a better idea than horror movies. Let's watch some of those paranormal documentaries."

Maybe she could learn something from one of them.

"Those are so cheesy."

Her dad rolled his eyes, but Bailey noticed his shoulders relax. He'd be happy they were spending time together, and Bailey could still work on some of the details of what she'd experienced.

"Bye, Hunter. Text me," she said, wishing she could kiss him goodbye.

But that would mean a night of third-degree questions, and maybe worse. Because by the looks of the sudden turnaround, her dad might try to relive his teenage years by commiserating about his experiences with girls.

Instead, she watched Hunter leave, hoping the ghost would leave him and his family alone. If it really was her it didn't like, he should be okay.

"Sorry we didn't decorate this year," Dad said as he poured out mugs of cider.

"That's cool. I would've done it if it was a big deal."

Bailey cupped the warm mug in her hands and inhaled. A cinnamon stick floated in the pot and she could smell it mixing with the sweet apple. This was Caleb's favorite fall treat. She'd never turn it down, though her preference was cocoa with marshmallows. Still, she smiled and appreciated the effort while following her dad back to the living room, with a giant bowl of popcorn and a plate of warm cookies. She could deal with that for dinner. She'd done worse, and her mom used to be the cook in the family, except for the baked goods which was Dad's department.

"So..." her father drew out the word, expectantly.

"So, what?" Bailey curled up in the corner of the sofa and reached for the remote.

"So... Hunter. I saw the way you two were looking at each other."

Bailey may as well have kissed him goodbye, because apparently she wasn't escaping the inquisition.

"He's cool. Hey, let's check out *Ghostly Guests* first." She tried to redirect her dad's attention to the menu on the flat screen. "See, the good thing about these shows is they're short, so if we hate it we can find another."

"Okay, Bailey, if you don't want to talk about your love life, fine. But I'm here if you need me, okay? I know I've been distant since... since Caleb." He looked down at his lap, where his hands twisted together. "And I'm sorry. You shouldn't be ignored."

Her father's voice was thick and Bailey knew he was holding back the grief, trying to be manly, which was such an ancient way of thinking.

She glanced over at the pile of pictures still on the coffee table. Without a word, Bailey got up and scooted in next to her father, where she nestled against his side and rested her head on his shoulder. His body began to shake before the sobs came. Bailey stayed there, huddled with her dad, who felt inhumanly frail as he finally let it out. At least, in front of Bailey.

After a while, he began to quiet and Bailey realized her own face was wet. Maybe the timing sucked, but Hunter was right. She needed this time with her dad.

"How about some *Ghostly Guests*?" her dad asked, with a stuffy nose.

"First order us some pizza," Bailey suggested. "This could be a long night."

CHAPTER 12

The morning sun slipped through the slats of the blinds, striping Bailey's face in shadow and light and irritating her awake. Her dad had retired to his room by midnight, and she'd pretended to be just as sleepy. Well, okay, maybe she wasn't *pretending* exactly, but she had things to do. She'd tried texting Hunter, and assumed by his silence that he was either asleep or his phone was being possessed again by whatever was in the house.

The first thing she needed was a hot shower, so she let the steam fill the bathroom while she once again thought through last night's research. There definitely were commonalities between all the ghost stories she'd seen and read online. Obviously, most were explainable, or made up by online attention seekers or people wanting ratings. But others... the people seemed so normal and didn't even want their names out there.

Bailey's Guide to the Paranormal
1. Usually the house or land was the site of a violent or confusing death.
2. All the senses can be triggered by the ghost. I have felt, seen, smelled, and heard it.
3. Most ghosts are harmless. Sadly, the knife-throwing and push-down-the-stairs one in the Gallows House seems to be of the rarer variety.
4. If the ghost was conscious and not what they called a residual haunting, they usually wanted something. So what does the Gallows Ghost want? And who is it?
5. Like Hunter pointed out, they feed off of energy. The more fear they elicit, the stronger they are.
6. They can interact with the living at will.

Bailey sighed as she turned off the shower and wrapped herself in a fluffy white towel. It still didn't explain what it had done to her brother to make him take his life.

"Who are you?" Bailey whispered, as she wiped the fogged mirror.

The sickeningly sweet smell of floral perfume filled the room and made her stomach swim. Had she accidentally knocked over a bottle of something? Bailey scanned the counter tops and saw nothing, but when she looked up again at the mirror, the steam behind her had formed into the outline of a woman, the same way as the one she'd seen at the bottom of the stairs when she was pushed.

Though her heart raced, Bailey forced herself to stay calm. This apparition had tried to help her get away. It wasn't the evil one, and the more she told herself to stay calm the more she realized she didn't feel threatened.

"Who are you?" she whispered again, this time trying hard not to blink lest the woman disappear.

The mirror had begun to fog up again and she was losing sight of the woman behind her. Just as she considered turning around, an invisible finger began to write on the surface.

I am, and a period. No, a dot.

"Dottie. Dorothy Radcliff?" Bailey asked, heart pounding now for a different reason.

The apparition nodded, and where there was no face, the semblance of one began to form.

"Oh, my God. I'm so sorry about what happened to you in the attic."

Bailey's insides began to squirm and it was more than merely Dottie's perfume. The specter began to shake her head, hollow eyes now formed, seeming somehow sad, something dark and amorphous shadowing her cheek. A bruise?

"I don't understand," Bailey said, wishing she could talk to her like a normal person. "Is the story wrong?"

The writing continued. *Not me.* Then as it faded, more words formed. *Find me.*

Bailey's head hurt. This was getting more confusing.

"If it's not you in the story, then who?" Bailey asked desperately, as the figure in the mirror began to fade.

After spinning around, Bailey found that the figure was gone. A blast of wind rushed past, pricking goosebumps along her exposed skin and whispering a name.

Susan.

***

Bailey threw on clothes and pulled a brush through her hair, leaving it wet and loose. She hurried downstairs and past her dad, to the front door.

"Where are you going so early and… wet?" her dad asked, from his spot on the sofa, with a mug of coffee.

"Report time. We want to get as much done as possible before tonight so we can take Hunter's little brother trick-or-treating." Bailey knew her smile was fake as hell, but hoped her dad would buy a reasonable enough explanation.

"I'm glad to see you hanging out with friends again, Bailey. Caleb would be happy, too."

A knot formed in the base of her throat as she nodded, not trusting her voice. Then she headed out and up Willow.

The crowd for the big day was visible from the moment she turned the corner. It was at least double the usual size, with various TV company vans lining the side of the street. About a hundred people pressed in against the property line, further than Bailey had ever seen them get.

Circumventing the hubbub, Bailey went to the other side of street and past the crowd. She moved to the house beyond Gallows and up the back of the property, where Hunter always slipped by in the morning to wait for her to walk to school.

She made it to the back porch, where she knocked on the door to the kitchen, hoping someone wouldn't only hear it, but know it wasn't one of the gawkers or some Halloween ghost groupie. A gust of wind passed her shoulder, making her hug her sweater to her body as her breath fogged out in front of her. And as it passed, the door creaked open as though blown inward. Bailey hesitated until a whiff of flowery perfume helped her understand it was Dottie who had opened the door. Feeling safer and more confident, she entered the house and immediately felt awkward. For all intents and purposes, she'd just broken into Hunter's house.

The heavenly scent of Estrella's baking and coffee helped ease her conscience and get past the memory of the last time she'd stood in that very room. She cleared her throat and called out as she made her way through the now tidy kitchen, toward the front room.

"Hello? It's Bailey. I came in the back because I couldn't get to the front door. Hope it's okay."

No one answered as she searched the first floor. With a deep breath and a lot of determination, she put a hand on the banister and climbed the staircase toward the second story landing. She continued to call out, intermittently. When she reached the top of the steps, she glanced both directions and decided to head the way she'd been that first day she'd visited the house. The door to the room where the paint had spilled was ajar, and a shiver went down her spine when she saw it remained deep burgundy instead of the intended sage green.

From the other end of the hallway, a door clicked shut and she spun, again calling out only to find no one there. The question was who or *what* had closed the door?

As Bailey stood pondering whether to head to the other, somehow darker, side of the hall, a hand grasped her shoulder and she twirled again, heart colliding with her ribs. She threw a hand over her chest when she saw Fynn standing behind her in a tight white T-shirt and low-hanging pajama pants.

"Oh, my God, you scared the crap out of me," she breathed.

"Sorry. But in my defense, you're the one upstairs in my house early on a Saturday morning." Fynn smiled his practiced grin and let his hands fall lightly to his sides.

"I've been calling out and searching for signs of life this whole time," she explained. "I need Hunter and he won't answer my texts."

Fynn clutched his chest like she'd stabbed him. "She chooses the geeky brother." Then he stood up, laughing a little. "He's probably asleep and didn't hear the phone. Feel free to wake him, though. I think Mom is probably out front trying to disperse the masses."

"There were so many this morning."

Bailey felt much better now that a human was having a rational conversation with her. Fynn was much better when he wasn't drunk.

"Halloween and all." Fynn snorted. "You're welcome to join me for some coffee and breakfast downstairs if you want to let lover boy sleep a bit longer."

"I really do need to talk to him," Bailey said, "but thanks, I do love your mom's food. Can you point me to the right room, please?"

Fynn put a hand on her shoulder and steered her toward the darker side of the hall. Of course. He gestured toward the last door in the corner, bathed in shadow, then leaned down and whispered in her ear.

"Tom is right across the hall, so don't make too much noise if you don't want to wake him."

Bailey wasn't sure if he was implying something or not, so she let it go, muttered a thanks, and headed for the corner door.

"Hey, Fynn," she called in a half-whisper.

He turned at the top of the stairs and raised his brows in question, his face scruffy with stubble.

"What's that door for?" She gestured to a slim, slightly raised door at the end of the hall, where she was sure the house stopped.

It was painted the same dark grey color as the walls to camouflage it.

Fynn shook his head. "Such a weird house. That goes to the attic." Then he padded down the steps and disappeared from sight.

Bailey stared at the door for a full minute before knocking lightly on Hunter's room. There was something so strange about it. So out of place that at some point someone had wanted to hide its existence.

When Hunter didn't answer, Bailey grabbed the handle and slowly peeked inside. The curtains were drawn and the old-fashioned four-poster sat across from it, reminding Bailey that the Callahans must've saved money on the furniture being included with the house. There was no way Hunter had picked out that heavy, ornate design.

On it, the plain blue comforter was crumpled and a long arm and leg stuck out the side and hung over the edge of the bed. Bailey couldn't help but smile as she moved over close enough to see his face, peeking out of the blanket, curly black hair spread over the pillow and mouth open. He looked like a little boy, lying there sound asleep, and she had an urge to climb in behind him and cuddle under the covers. But they had work to do, and now she knew it was for more than Caleb's sake. It was for Dottie and the mysterious Susan, and anyone else who the house may try to claim in the future.

"Morning, sleepy head." She leaned down over Hunter's head.

He blinked slowly and opened his eyes, and she watched the joy spread over his face as consciousness crept in, revealing what was happening.

"Bailey?" he asked, voice cracking from sleep.

"That's me."

Her hair, now mostly dry, hung on either side of her face and coiled onto the blankets.

Before she knew what was happening, Hunter reached up and pulled her down onto the bed with him, tangling her in the blankets and his arms and legs. She laughed and squealed, trying to keep as quiet as possible to not wake Tom. And she had to admit, it felt amazing to lie in a pile of cloudlike puffiness, face to face with Hunter, warm and happy in his arms.

"Is it my birthday?" he asked, groggily.

"It's Halloween," she said, still laughing. "And I've been trying to get ahold of you again."

"Well, if that means you showing up in my room, I may have to deactivate my cell."

Hunter smothered her giggles with a kiss, and in moments their tangle on the bed became heated and electric. He threw the comforter over them, drowning their bodies, heads and all in darkness, and there was only Hunter and Bailey.

When Estrella knocked on the door a few minutes later, Hunter threw the blanket off their heads, popping their momentary bubble of happiness and letting in a rush of cold air.

"*Mijo*," Estrella called through the door. "Is Bailey with you? Fynn said she's here."

Hunter jumped up as quiet as a mouse and pulled a crumpled pair of jeans on from the floor in such record time that Bailey wondered if he'd had practice.

"I'm here, Mrs. Callahan," Bailey called, slipping out of the bed as well and raking her fingers through her knotted mess of hair.

Moments later, Bailey opened the door, hoping she wasn't terribly flushed and that Hunter'd had enough time to cool off.

"Sorry." She offered Estrella one of her patented forced smiles. "I guess the door closed. I didn't mean for it to appear inappropriate."

Bailey glanced back at Hunter, who sat on the bed, hugging a pillow like he'd just woken up. He was probably hiding his lap, which made her blush even more.

"These doors are constantly closing on their own," Estrella said, with a warm and maybe too understanding smile. "Come downstairs and have some coffee and a muffin. I want to apologize for what happened last time you were here. I felt terrible."

Bailey remembered the fear that coursed through her when she was pushed down the stairs, and she squared her shoulders, embarrassed once again that she'd let it chase her from the house and the amazing family that lived in it.

"I'm the one who should apologize, Mrs. Callahan. I never should've run off like that."

"Estrella. And we'll consider it forgotten."

She opened up her arms and Bailey accepted a hug filled with the comforting scent of fresh-baked sweets.

"I am hungry," Hunter said, joining them at the door as Tom opened his own, across the way, rubbing tired eyes.

"Did someone say food?" Tom asked. "Oh, hi, Bailey."

"Hi," Bailey said and accepted Hunter's hand as they all walked downstairs.

"I'd love some help preparing the sweet bread for tomorrow," Estrella said after they'd filled themselves with cinnamon muffins, warm from the oven.

Bailey cupped her mug of cocoa, inhaling the aroma of dark chocolate and cream.

"We have to work on a report for school." Hunter found her knee, under the table.

"Alone in your room?" Tom asked with a smirk.

Estrella hushed him and shooed him upstairs to shower and dress so he could help her.

"Then you best get to work," she said. "School is important. When you get hungry, I'll have some soup and sandwiches ready for lunch."

Bailey rose and set her mug in the sink. "I can't thank you enough for being so welcoming, Estrella."

"Nonsense. I want my home to feel like home to all our friends."

With a warm and wistful feeling, Bailey followed Hunter out into the hall.

"She likes you," Hunter said, pulling her in close.

"I'm glad. I like her, too. Your whole family is amazing." Bailey beamed up at this boy who'd captured her heart so quickly.

"Glad you think so," he said and leaned in for a slow and tender kiss.

"We really do need to work," Bailey groaned.

"Okay. Where do we start?" Hunter looked around. "It's been awfully quiet this morning. I wonder what that means."

Bailey shrugged. "I was thinking that, too. I suspect maybe it has to do with the good ghost watching out for us." She then explained about Dottie and her experience that morning.

"You know, if you'd told me that story a month ago, I would've thought you were cute but insane."

"Now?" asked Bailey, amused by the nearly hidden compliment.

"Now, I really appreciate Dottie."

Bailey finally acknowledged what she'd known since that morning but hadn't wanted to admit to herself.

She braced herself. "I know what we have to do."

"What?"

"We have to go up in the attic."

CHAPTER 13

The grin on Hunter's face morphed into a hard line.

"We have to figure out who it was that died up there," Bailey said. "If it wasn't Dottie. And we need to find Dottie. She asked me to, and I feel like I owe her because she tried to save me from getting hurt." Bailey squeezed Hunter's hands, trying to ignore the pounding in her chest when she thought about climbing into the attic.

"We've never been up there," Hunter said as they slowly climbed the stairs.

"What?" Bailey stopped halfway to the landing. "How can there be a place in your house you've never been?"

She didn't really need an answer. This wasn't an ordinary house and the mere idea of going up there filled her with dread. She drew a deep breath then followed with the question she'd really meant to ask.

"Are you sure?" Because as silly as that sounded, she remembered clear as day having seen someone up there watching her from the window. The dark silhouette of a man, who at the time she'd assumed was one of them. But now that she thought about it, she'd reasoned it was Hunter's father, who wasn't in the picture.

"Well, yeah," Hunter replied, clearly confused. "What's up?"

Bailey forced herself to continue up the steps, though with each one she climbed, the harder it got. Everything in her was screaming at her to turn and run the other way. Even the air felt thicker on the second story landing.

"I think there's a reason no one wants to go up there. I don't think he wants us up there."

Hunter didn't need to ask who *he* was. They both knew they were dealing with some insane ghost, and it was almost certainly a male. Whether it was Basil or Artemis or some unknown entity, she didn't know. A few of the shows she'd watched the night before determined the evil was caused by a demon, and Bailey didn't even want to contemplate that thought.

"I wish there was a weapon we could use on a ghost," Hunter said, leading her down the hall in the opposite direction than she'd expected.

"I thought that door near your room went up to the attic."

"Does it? Yeah, probably. It doesn't make sense for it to go anywhere else. But as far as I know, it's sealed. Besides, this should work, too."

Reaching up on his toes and stretching upward, Hunter's fingers barely scraped the handle on the hatch in the ceiling, but he finally managed to coax it down. They backed up as an old wooden stepladder slipped downward with a creek, shooting a cloud of dust out like a bomb. Bailey coughed, turning her head into her elbow, as Hunter waved his hands in front of them to clear the air. Once the dust and debris had settled, they stepped forward.

"Let me go first." Hunter stopped her with a hand on her shoulder.

Bailey wordlessly agreed. Not because she wanted a man to protect her, but because of the rats and spiders that no doubt resided in the unused attic of a previously abandoned house. She followed close behind and they held out their phones with the flashlights on. When Hunter poked his head above the top of the opening, he paused, swinging the light in a large arc.

"What do you see?" Bailey asked.

"An attic." Hunter finished climbing out before turning to give her a hand up.

"Very funny," Bailey said, brushing the dirt from her knees. It took only a second for her to note the faint stench of something rotten in the still air.

They shone their lights around the room, catching thick layers of dust and spiderwebs hanging from every corner. The space itself was huge, spanning the length of the house without the walls to divide it into rooms. Thick beams of wood hung from the ceiling, which tapered up in the center in a deep, upside-down V-shape. Made sense, considering the sharply sloping roof on the house. Also made it difficult to stand at the outskirts of the attic without hitting your head, especially Hunter. The center length of the attic, however, had more space than Bailey would have imagined, and the beams crisscrossing at the top made her wonder if bats hid in the crevices.

Various boxes and trunks were stacked at odd angles on the outskirts, while pieces of old furniture and strange knickknacks filled the spaces between. Webs ran from the tops of various things, at angles up toward the cathedral-like ceiling. Straight down the way, at the center of the highest point, was the enormous lead-lined window where Bailey had seen what she thought had been a man from outside. She realized now that, proportionally, the figure had to have been at least eight feet tall, and that made her heart seize up.

Not much light filtered through inside the attic, which was strange and unnerving. It was sunny outside, yet the inside was filled with shadows. Though the outlines of things were clear now that her eyes had adjusted, the lights from their phones still helped quite a bit.

"Now what?" Hunter whispered.

Bailey understood the urge not to disturb anything—as weird as it was, not even the silence—so she too answered in hushed tones. "Well, where's the location they found the body?" she asked and wished again she'd been able to find the book.

"I'm thinking, over there." Hunter swung his light to an area a few feet from Bailey's left side.

Two chains dangled from a ceiling beam, ending in what looked like shackles. Bailey felt like an elephant sat on her chest. The thick, rusted chains swung lightly as though there was a breeze in the stuffy and still attic.

"It's moving," Hunter said.

At least he was still able to speak.

Bailey forced air into her body so she wouldn't pass out as she pictured discovering the skeleton swinging there, feet inches above the ground. Between her imagination, the smell, and the stuffiness, the muffin in her stomach threatened to make an unexpected appearance.

"Let's start over there." Hunter pulled her toward the chains.

The ground beneath them was stained with something dark that Bailey didn't want to think too much about, and there were scratches in the wood as well.

"Probably rats looking for food," Hunter said, when he saw what she was looking at, which really didn't help.

Bailey began with a box that sat below and to the right. She dragged it toward her and began rifling through old papers and books from the 1960's. Everything was fragile and yellowed with age. Hunter pulled out a box from the other side and did the same.

After about an hour of searching through useless packages of clothing, bedding, and papers, Bailey kicked the last container from frustration. She hadn't known what she was looking for, but she was sure there was something up there that she was supposed to find.

Hunter dropped the file he was looking through and came over to pull her into his arms. That's when she got another good look at the floor. She saw the marks the boxes had made when they'd dragged them away to search through. And she saw the scratches on the stained ground beneath the chains. An area they'd left alone, since it felt sacred.

"Look at that." Bailey pointed at it. "Those aren't rat scratches. Those are marks of something heavy being dragged through whatever was on the floor."

Hunter followed as she pointed, tracing the trajectory of the lines that were clearly old. She ended up at a pile of boxes lying on and around an ancient-looking trunk made of cedar and bronze.

"That's where we look next," Bailey said triumphantly. "Help me move those boxes."

Together, they worked until the area was clear and they'd uncovered the treasure chest about four-feet by two-feet, with a rounded top. The thick copper clasp, dulled by time and dust, seemed formidable, but Bailey knew she was getting some kind of answer from within and she wouldn't stop until she figured it out.

"We need something heavy to break it open." Hunter contemplated the lock.

"Did you try it?" Bailey asked with a smirk. She knew it was doubtful, but hey—the path of least resistance was usually the right one.

Hunter shot her a wry look from beneath his mop of hair and tugged at it. The moment he did, the door they'd climbed up through slammed shut, and a huge wind barreled through the entire space of the attic with a horrifying howl, kicking up dirt and debris. Bailey screamed and covered her face with her arm as Hunter threw his own over her, pulling her down with him behind the trunk and close to the floor as their backs were pummeled by bits of long forgotten past.

"We have to get out of here," Hunter yelled.

Despite being so close to Bailey's ear, the angry howl of the tornado still nearly drowned him out.

"He's trying to stop us from opening the chest." Bailey screeched back.

She kept one hand firmly on the side of it, not willing to abandon what she was surer than ever held important clues. No sooner than she had cemented her intentions, strong arms wrapped themselves around her waist and yanked her up and away from Hunter. At first, she thought it must be Fynn, trying to save her or something stupid, but judging by the horror-stricken look on Hunter's face, it was nothing so normal.

"Let go!" she yelled and kicked at the air. Before she could react further, she was flying with the wind, sailing so fast that her stomach couldn't keep up. She knew she was about to hit the window as it rushed toward her with blinding speed. Hunter's desperate calls and footfalls echoed in her mind, but there was no way he would make it in time. She would collide with the leaded glass. She was about to die.

Then three things happened at once. Screams tore at Bailey's throat as she threw her hands out in front of her to try to halt the collision. The wind died, and something large and heavy crashed behind her field of view. The glowing apparition of a woman with red hair and a flowing dress appeared between her and the window. The ghost opened her arms as her eyes glowed like orbs of pure light. It felt to Bailey as if two equally strong forces were trying to pull her body in opposite directions at once. Pain crashed over her in waves as she slowed, hovered in mid-air, and finally fell in a heap on the ground.

She lay still for a minute in the sudden silence, hair over her face, preventing her from seeing the aftermath of the attack. Her breath came ragged and heavy, her chest and throat hurting with each gasp like she'd run a marathon in record time.

"Bailey."

She heard Hunter call her name, soft and frightened like a small boy. She felt his hand ever so softly on her back.

"Are you okay?"

Was she? Bailey took stock of her body. As far as she could tell, she was sore like she'd had the workout of her life. She was nauseous, dizzy, and confused—but alive. That wasn't a warning. It was an attempt on her life. If that other ghost hadn't shown up, she'd have smashed through the window, three stories up, at an insane velocity.

Bailey nodded because she couldn't find her voice. She let Hunter help her shakily to her feet and wrap an arm around her for support. She didn't know if she really was hurt or merely in shock, but she nonetheless leaned on his strong, lithe frame as he slowly led her past a pile of spilled papers and boxes, to the trap door. Before he could set her down on a box still standing, the door sprung open and the stairs slid down like they'd just been oiled.

She didn't want to go. She didn't want to give up. But with one last longing look toward the chest, now buried once again in clutter, Bailey followed Hunter down to the second floor.

CHAPTER 14

They made it back to Hunter's room before Bailey lost it. Hunter simply held her in his arms as she cried, face pressed against his chest, his chin on her head. When she finished with being a blubbering idiot, Bailey wiped her face on her arm and separated herself enough to sit on the bed, still not willing to look Hunter in the face. She wasn't sure what she'd find there. Would he refuse to let her search anymore? Did he think she was weak?

"I've never seen anything like that," Hunter said, and she finally glanced at him.

He was pale and wide-eyed, hands trembling in his lap. She hadn't even noticed.

"It was like something plucked you off the ground like a speck of dust, and hurtled you toward the window. I couldn't catch you." He shook his head, staring at nothing, like he was watching it on replay. "Then you stopped. In mid-air, and hovered for a second, and... boom. You were dropped like a rag doll."

"Someone stopped him from throwing me through the window," Bailey said, voice steadier than she felt. "It was a woman."

"Dottie?" Hunter asked.

"No. This lady had red hair. Dottie's pictures all show a brunette. Plus, I don't know, the face looked different, even though Dottie's wasn't that clear when I saw her."

"So, this was another woman who died in the house?" Hunter reasoned. "Who had red hair?"

"I wish we had that book," Bailey said, angered that it was still gone.

"I'll order a new one." Hunter took out his phone.

Even though Bailey didn't stop him, she knew it wasn't enough. It was something in her brother's notes that held the key. It had disappeared for a reason and it bothered her more than she wanted to admit, that it had reached all the way to her house to take it. That meant she was as vulnerable at home as she was in this house.

A terrible thought occurred to her for the first time. It was so horrible that the blood in her veins felt like it froze.

"What is it? What's wrong?" Hunter asked.

"What if Caleb didn't kill himself?" she whispered. "What if something else pulled the trigger and made it look like a suicide?"

"We can't keep using conjecture to figure things out," Hunter said, softly. "There's no point in picturing things like that unless we have more information. It'll tear you apart. Believe me, I know."

"How do you know?" Bailey snapped, fresh tears stinging her eyes.

He had never even *met* Caleb.

"You have no idea how many times I imagined my dad being cleared of all charges. I was sure he was framed, that it was a police mistake, that it was someone that looked like him, just not him, because it couldn't have been him that did that horrible thing. But no matter how much I denied it, reality was reality."

Bailey stood sharply, chest aching with the effort it was taking not to snap at him. He was hurting, that was clear, and she could picture him, a little boy, pained and confused by someone he loved that had left him behind. But Caleb wasn't his father. He wasn't a felon and he didn't kill anyone. He couldn't have. He wouldn't have left her the way Hunter's father had left them.

"I should go home," she said, hugging herself.

"You don't have to." Hunter peered through the slats of his blinds toward the front. "They're still out there. Maybe they plan to stay until tonight. I don't know what they think will happen just because it's Halloween."

"Charity keeps texting me," Bailey explained, holding up the phone she'd left in Hunter's room like evidence. "She says she has something for me and wants us to meet tonight to work on the paper."

The truth was, Bailey could write a nine-page essay about the Gallows House with her eyes closed at this point.

"Let's do it." Hunter scrunched his face into a determined scowl. "Let's meet tonight somewhere and write it all out. Maybe we'll see something new when we do. In the meantime, I'll research ways to get rid of ghosts."

Bailey sniffed. "Somehow, I don't think anything short of an exorcism by the Pope himself is going to do the trick. Be careful if you decide to burn extra sage, because in at least half the shows I saw last night, that either worked for like two days or made it angrier."

Hunter grinned and leaned down to kiss her goodbye. Bailey turned so that his lips landed on the top of her head, then slipped out the door and headed down the steps.

Pausing near the kitchen door, Bailey listened to the sound of Estrella humming as she worked, and inhaled deeply, drawing in the scent of the sweet bread and cinnamon. Had Estrella also believed her husband innocent? Was it possible to love someone so much that you were blind to who they really were? With what felt like bricks in her stomach, Bailey said a quick and cheerful goodbye to Estrella and slipped out the backdoor.

The air outside felt lighter, but the bricks didn't disappear as Bailey stole through the yard and to the street. A chill wind whipped at her hair and she pulled her sweater tighter around herself as the intensity of the morning played on repeat in her mind. Everything from the heat and joy of making out with Hunter in his bed, to the terror of being thrown toward the window in the attic. To thoughts and questions about Caleb's death.

Her phone buzzed and she pulled it out, clearing her vision with a swipe of her sleeve. After seeing Charity's frantic texts, Bailey finally answered. What she wasn't expecting was her friend to be waiting for her at the door with a manic smile and a big black and orange shopping bag.

"What's all this?" Bailey asked, grateful to feed off her friend's enthusiasm.

"Our costumes," Charity squealed.

Bailey blinked.

"I know," Charity said, pushing past Bailey on her way in the house. "We didn't discuss it this year, so I thought I'd take something off your plate. You're welcome."

"What are we?"

"You're a cat." Charity shoved a bundle of black into Bailey's chest. "I know what you're thinking. Cliché, right? Well, fear not, because it's not just a cat. Wait for it…"

"Please don't say sex kitten."

Charity giggled. "Nice. But no. You're my familiar. I'm a witch and your collar matches my dress. See?" She rummaged in the bag until she pulled out a cute red and black witch's outfit. "Unless you want to be the witch? I don't mind switching, but I'm not sure the bodysuit will fit me."

Bodysuit? Bailey unfolded the mass she had clutched to her chest, and found a tiny black bodysuit, red and black jeweled collar, and a bedazzled red and black cat mask with ruby-studded ears poking up and whiskers poking out on either side of the nose.

"I was thinking you could wear those high leather boots you wore when you were Wonder Woman two years ago," Charity said.

She might as well be a sex kitten.

"What do you think? You're so quiet." Charity bit her lower lip and waited with wide eyes.

"It's really cute. Thanks for doing this for me."

Leave it to Charity to take care of her. Although she wasn't in the spirit of the season, she knew Halloween was such a big deal in Shadow Springs that the majority of the town dressed up to celebrate, adults and children alike.

"So, what's the plan?" Charity bounced up Bailey's staircase.

It seemed Bailey's dad was nowhere to be found.

"We're meeting Hunter to work on the paper," she said, though she wasn't sure that was what she ought to be spending her time on. What she really wanted was to find Caleb's book and get back in that attic to open the mysterious chest.

"Not in the house?" Charity asked.

"We're meeting here. Hunter's is going to be a madhouse. There're already a gazillion people camping outside for no real reason."

"Well, I'll text Leah, but I'm pretty sure she's going to protest." Charity whipped out her bubblegum-pink-cased phone and typed for a bit, paused and typed again, mouth hanging open. "She's busy." Charity smirked.

"Doing?" Bailey asked, only half-interested. Frankly she didn't care if Leah couldn't make it.

"She's going out with Fynn."

"What?" Anger heated the back of Bailey's neck.

Charity waved her phone, then stuck it back in her pocket.

Whatever. She finally figured out she couldn't flirt her way in through Hunter, so she moved on.

"He's an adult," Bailey said, still fuming. "It's wrong."

"He's only a year or so older than her. It's not that big of a deal," Charity said then pulled off her shirt to change.

"Not a big deal?" Bailey repeated, appalled. "Did you not see him the other night? In the back of a police car?"

Charity shrugged. "Since when do you care so much about Leah? Besides, Fynn would be an idiot to do anything remotely inappropriate now."

Bailey kept her mouth shut while she changed. It was silly of her to be so offended by Leah and Fynn dating. What did she care? She wasn't jealous. She preferred Hunter's gentleness and patience to Fynn's bravado and need to be the center of attention. And it was better that Leah was out of their hair, right? Still, she figured she should give Hunter a heads-up, and decided to shoot him a quick text as soon as she was able.

Bailey filled Charity in on the situation with the house and the haunting. She knew Charity wouldn't doubt her, not just because she'd grown up in Shadow Springs, but also because she was the loyal friend that had been there for Bailey all along, never once questioning her desire to find a connection between the Gallows House and Caleb's death.

"Are you sure you're okay?" Charity asked, when she finished.

Bailey nodded but wrung her hands a lot like her dad did when he was upset.

"So I'm going to skip over the whole being hurt that you didn't tell me, because I'll assume you were wanting time alone with Hunter. What can I do to help?"

Bailey hugged her friend, now in full witch's garb.

"Not much, unless you can figure out how to get me safely in the attic to open the trunk," she said, over Charity's shoulder. "Or can figure out where a ghost might hide a book."

"Hmm. Have you tried the Internet?"

"Well, yes and no," Bailey stammered. "I mean, not today."

"Let's hit the library." Charity bounced enough that her little puffy skirt flounced along with her. "We can look for another copy of the book so we at least have half the info, and we can search online for new info, too. We'll gather enough to bring it to the meeting with Hunter later, and together we can exorcise that asshole ghost into the ether." She made an exploding sound that she accented with her hands.

"You make it sound easy."

"Sometimes you're too close to see how easy it is."

"Let's go," Bailey said, feeling hopeful again as she tugged on the boots she'd had tucked in the corner of her closet for two years. "But we have to make one stop on the way."

"What's that?"

"Food. I need some fries and a shake. You know, brain food."

Charity and Bailey laughed, linking arms like when they were younger and carefree. They stumbled down the steps in their heels just as Bailey's dad came home with arms full of candy. As they said their goodbyes to him, Bailey couldn't help but feel some of the old excitement of Halloweens gone by.

CHAPTER 15

Hunter never answered her text, and by the time they were through, Bailey decided they had to take the Willow road detour home. Armed with books and bags from the kind of local stores that depended on Halloween for their main income, they walked toward the Gallows House.

If Bailey and Charity looked out of place, it was because they weren't weird enough compared to the crowd camped out on the grounds of the home. A small group of hooded figures surrounded the great willow tree in the front, linking hands, with large black candles burning at the base. Bailey felt uneasy.

"That could catch on fire," Charity said, pointing at the circle of thirteen people.

That was merely one of the many horrible possibilities that had passed through Bailey's mind. She was debating whether to approach them, when sirens peeled around the corner from the direction of her house. Sure enough, two police cars pulled up, scattering some of the onlookers and throwing their lights into the mix. Out climbed the same officers from the other night, and Sergeant Harper held up a megaphone.

"Step away from the grounds. This is private property and the homeowner will press charges against anyone who trespasses."

He moved forward, the other officer following, hand on holster, eyes shifting to keep everyone in sight. Harper repeated his announcement, successfully scattering the would-be devil worshippers or whoever they were. Everyone else backed up, giving the sidewalk a wide berth. Bailey took Charity's hand and pulled her forward, package and books in tow, just as she'd had to since turning the corner. Bailey didn't think Charity was doing it on purpose, but she did suspect some internal drive was telling her to stay as far away as possible.

Harper was already bending over to extinguish the candles, and Bailey knelt next to him to help. She noticed an abandoned Ouija board on the grass not far from the tree.

"Miss Thompson. I assume you heard my announcement?" Harper said jovially as Charity came around to join them.

"Sure did. Thanks, Sergeant. I wasn't sure how to handle that." Bailey blew out the last remaining light.

"You don't." Harper took hold of her shoulder and looked her straight in the eyes with his own ice blue ones. "You understand that? You don't *handle* anything yourself. You call me. I'm serious, Miss Thompson."

"Yes, sir." Bailey reached for the old board game gone awry.

Before she could touch it, the planchette jerked to life and began to slide, slowly at first, then picking up speed. Bailey yelped and leapt backward, hitting Harper's shoulder as they all watched. The planchette's path was anything but natural as it swirled and paused to point out each specific letter.

O—U—T.

When it finished the final letter, the planchette began to spin, faster and faster, along with the beat of Bailey's heart. When she was sure it would burn a hole in the board, it flew up and off, forcing Charity to duck. It impaled itself in the trunk of the willow, at about head height.

They all stared for a full minute.

"Did you girls, uh, see that too?" Harper finally asked.

Charity nodded, eyes wide.

"It could have been a prank," Bailey suggested, unsure why she was protecting him from the truth.

"Pretty elaborate," Harper muttered, stooping to pick up the board and examine it for wires and such.

"Well, we better be going," Bailey said, tugging Charity toward the porch. "We have to get Hunter. We have… Halloween plans."

Harper waved them off, preoccupied with his examination, which Bailey knew would turn up nothing.

"Are you sure we should be here?" Charity whispered, as Bailey rang the old bell. "It said to leave."

"All the more reason to get Hunter out of there and figure out how to get rid of the thing that's dangerous." Bailey stared at the door, willing it to open.

Finally, it did, and a harried-looking Estrella stood in the gaping maw of the entryway, appearing smaller than usual. Still, she smiled warmly upon seeing Bailey.

"Come in." Estrella motioned for them to enter. "I'm so glad it's you, dear. I was afraid one of those people had gotten too brave." She glared out past Bailey's shoulder as she ushered her inside. "I called the cops on them."

"They're here. I'm Charity Morgan, a friend of Hunter and Bailey's, from school." She stuck out her hand in greeting.

"Pleased to meet you." Estrella took her hand to shake. "I'm Estrella."

Bailey waited as Charity let her gaze flow over the immense darkness of the room, covered from floor to ceiling in wood paneling and detailed accents. Then to the winding staircase with worn burgundy carpeting flowing over the steps that Bailey had been pushed down. Her friend took in the old dusty furniture that came with the house—everything from the enormous Grandfather clock that long ago became stuck at 3:13, to the velvet couches and chairs. Then beyond that to the myriad of doors that blended with the paneling and created a puzzle-like effect.

"Wow," Charity said. "Something smells amazing."

Estrella's face lit up. "It's for tomorrow, but why don't you girls taste it and tell me what you think? I'll call Hunter down and you can test it out while you wait."

The tiny woman shuffled to the foot of the steps, leaned one hand on the edge of the banister, and yelled up for Hunter. Then with one more smile, she disappeared into the kitchen, humming an almost-familiar tune.

"What a juxtaposition," Charity said, setting the books down next to the package, where Bailey had dumped it on the ottoman to the left.

"Juxtaposition?" Bailey repeated, amused.

"I mean, this sweet lady and the heavenly cooking compared to the big spooky mansion."

"Yeah. It gives us even more incentive to get rid of this thing terrorizing the place." Bailey didn't mention to her friend how the ghost seemed to leave the Callahan family alone and focus all its attention on her. If she said it out loud, it would freak her out even more.

By the time Hunter came galloping down the stairs, the girls were seated comfortably on the couch, eating conchas and spicy cocoa and laughing along with Estrella, at old family stories about Hunter as a little boy running naked through the house.

"Speaking of the adorable little behind," Estrella said with a wide grin and motioned for Hunter for join them.

"Mama, you didn't." Hunter's face darkened considerably.

Bailey's toes curled, remembering her time in the bed with him that morning. It was all so confusing. She was hurt about his comparison of his father to Caleb, but she couldn't deny the feelings she had for him. She'd just have to make him understand who Caleb was. She wouldn't give up on Hunter that easily. So when he plopped down next to her and took her hand, she accepted with a squeeze.

"That's my cue to go back to baking," Estrella said. "I hope you girls will stay for dinner. I have a special Halloween dinner planned, and then you can all take Tom out trick-or-treating while I set up the alter."

"Oh, we're kind of busy with schoolwo—" Bailey started.

"Sounds great," Charity cut in. "What's the alter for?"

Bailey stared at her friend, open-mouthed, as Estrella explained the Dia De Los Muertos tradition.

"We believe the dead walk the earth," Estrella said, in such a jovial way it was incongruous. "We put up an alter with the picture of a loved one who's passed on, and various other things to help lead them to us so we can visit."

"Cool," Charity said.

Estrella patted her cheek, then disappeared behind the kitchen door.

"What?" Charity said, upon seeing Bailey's face. "She's sooo nice. And wow, if dinner is half as good as these pastry things, then forget tiny chocolate bars and jolly ranchers."

Bailey laughed and rolled her eyes, but she did have to admit that Estrella's cooking was worth staying in the haunted house for dinner. Besides, now that Charity was in on everything, she had renewed confidence that they could attack the attic again. Strength in numbers, after all.

Another part of her tried not to focus on the idea that it would be easier for the dead to partake in the world of the living. She didn't want to get her hopes up about Caleb or worry about who else may be in the house.

"Doesn't Tom want to go out with his friends tonight?" Bailey asked Hunter, who was busy playing with her fingers, interlaced with his.

"Yeah, he does, but our mother won't let him go on his own yet. It's a sore spot. Though, I guess he agreed his senior-in-high-school brother would be cool enough to bring along."

"Plus, two hot girls," Charity said, standing to twirl in her costume. "Show him, Bailey."

Bailey shook her head but stood up to twirl for him, lowering the mask from on top of her head down onto her face. She finished with a *meow* and a fake cat-scratching motion toward Hunter, who laughed.

"I didn't get the memo," he said, looking down at his usual T-shirt and baggy jeans. "I need a costume."

"We took care of that," Charity announced, grabbing the bag she had set down.

She rummaged through and came out with the one they'd decided on together.

"I love it," Hunter said, holding it up in front of himself.

He disappeared upstairs for about five minutes and returned at the landing, where he cleared his throat loudly. Bailey looked up to find a magician at the top of steps, cape tossed over one shoulder, top hat askew. He wore a black button-down shirt tucked into black pants, and the cheesy black wand with white tips they'd bought, he tossed back and forth from one gloved hand to the other.

Bailey gave a wolf whistle as he bounded down the steps. She cuddled into his side beneath his arm and leaned against him, inhaling his familiar scent. Charity was seated on the couch, legs tucked up at an angle and nose buried in a book, obviously on purpose.

"So, is this your fantasy?" Hunter asked in a low tone, breath hot against her ear.

"It is now," she replied, following up with a kiss where her mask bumped the rim of his hat.

"Ahem," Fynn called from the stairs. He was dressed for Halloween, too, in a sexy cop outfit, obviously rented from one of the shops in town. "My shirt looks good on you, little bro."

"Thanks." Hunter pulled Bailey against his side.

Tom came down a minute later, dressed adorably as a gangster, complete with fedora and two-toned shoes. He grinned widely when he saw Bailey and Charity.

"You coming with us?" he asked.

"You bet," Bailey said. "I haven't gone in a few years. It'll be fun."

"Can I say you're my girlfriend?"

Bailey blanched.

"Too late. She's taken," Hunter said.

Bailey glanced up shyly, face warm.

"Right?" he asked.

"You bet."

Charity groaned from the couch. "I have a toothache from the sugar overload."

The doorbell rang then, and all heads shot upwards toward the front entrance. The only one who seemed nonplused was Fynn, who jogged over to open it. Bailey had almost forgotten about the crazy people outside, and nearly yelled at him to stop, but caught herself at the last second.

The door swung open to reveal Leah in a bright red corset and leather pants with a devil's tail poking out. Her hair was teased out in loose waves with a horned headband on top. Her makeup was laid on thick, her eyes rimmed in black liner that made them look huge, and her pouty lips a deep blood-red that matched the rest of her outfit, down to the stilettos on her feet. Over her shoulder was a big black tote bag, pulling down against her hip from a heavy load.

"Well, well," she said and came inside to hang on Fynn in a way that mirrored Bailey and Hunter's stance. "Looks like there really was a party at the house, and I wasn't invited."

"It wasn't planned," Bailey blurted out. "We were supposed to meet at my house—"

"Don't worry your pretty little head." Leah turned Fynn's face toward hers with a long-nailed hand. "I definitely got the better brother in the deal."

Bailey squeezed Hunter tighter around the waist, afraid he'd attack his brother or something, but he snorted instead.

"Dinner." Estrella called, from the kitchen doorway. "I thought we'd eat in the dining room."

Everyone trailed behind her to another door off to the left, across from a guest bathroom. The walls were paneled halfway up, and the oblong room was filled with the largest dining table Bailey had ever seen. It looked like it belonged at a castle in England in the 1500s, with its four-inch-thick top and high-backed chairs.

Estrella seemed not to notice, and carried her tray to the head of the table, where there were already seven places set, taking up less than a third of the room available. She sat at the head without ceremony, and began spooning what looked like individually wrapped tamales, onto her plate. There were steaming bowls of rice and beans also already set out, along with a pitcher of water.

"When did you do all this?" Bailey felt awful that she hadn't seen her and offered to help.

Estrella merely smiled and gestured to her guests to sit. Tom sat at his mom's side, Fynn next to him. Leah took the seat directly next to Fynn, and Bailey moved across from them, between Hunter and Charity. The food was wonderful, and thankfully Leah didn't make any more awkward comments. So other than draping herself over Fynn, she behaved normally.

"Thank you for dinner." Bailey leaned back in the chair and patted her stomach.

"You're welcome," Estrella said, standing to clear the table.

"Let us help you," Charity offered, standing also.

"Nonsense." Estrella said. "You are my guests. You sit and enjoy the company. I have to get back to cooking, anyway."

"Is that all she does?" Charity asked as Estrella balanced the dishes expertly on one tray.

"She loves it," Fynn said. "It's her happy place."

"Ours too," Hunter said, then also patted his nonexistent stomach.

He must have an amazing metabolism.

"I brought a little after-dinner entertainment." Leah gave a look that matched her outfit.

"What's that?" Fynn's arm was draped over her, even as she reached in her black bag.

"Tada." She pulled out a bottle of wine, and then a Ouija board.

"No way," Hunter said.

"Not again," Charity said, before Bailey could get her mouth working.

"Again?" Leah asked.

Bailey recounted their experience out on the lawn.

"Then we're definitely playing!" Leah clapped a little.

"No, you're not." Hunter stood.

"Relax," Fynn said, sitting up straight. "It's only a game."

"Mama would have a fit," Hunter hissed, tendons in his neck standing at attention. "Think about what you're doing."

"If you're worried about Mama, then don't tell her," Fynn said, dryly.

Tom stood and moved behind his brother and Leah, toward the exit. "Let's get out of here and go trick-or-treating before they summon a demon or something."

"I'm with him," Charity said, standing as well and tugging down her costume.

"Hunter?" Bailey asked, pulling at his arm that felt like stone.

"It's on you," Hunter said to Fynn, glaring at the bottle of wine on the table between them, and followed the others out of the room. "We promised to take Tom out."

"Are you going to tell your mom?" Bailey asked, as soon as they'd crossed the threshold.

Hunter stared back toward the dining room for a minute, face as hard-lined as the rest of him.

"No," he said, finally. It would only upset her, and I have a feeling Leah would get her way somehow. If it's that important to her, well, maybe she'll change her mind after she gets what she wants. He just better stay strong when it comes to the wine."

Bailey took one last worried glance toward the door, where she could still hear Leah giggling, then followed the others out.

CHAPTER 16

Watching Tom and his friends rush up to doors after weaving their way through the crowded streets, was fun. When they got to Bailey's house, her dad was sure to give them fistfuls of chocolates, happy to see his daughter out having a good time.

Charity reached into Tom's bag and snatched out a candy. He smiled at her as he rushed off with his friends, toward the next house.

"This is better than I remembered," Charity said.

"We have work to do." Bailey was picturing the things they'd left in the Gallows House. "We need to get back into the attic."

"No way." Hunter stopped in his tracks, nearly knocking her off her feet.

"We have precautions," Charity told him. "We were researching all afternoon, and we brought a few things with us that might offer some protection."

"Like sage?" Hunter asked sarcastically. "Because remember how well that turned out with the paint?"

"You picked that on purpose?" Bailey asked.

She hadn't realized that even then Hunter had accepted what was in his home.

"Mama did." He stared at his feet.

"We do have some bundles," Charity said. "But that's not all. We also have obsidian and quartz."

"And some crosses," Bailey said.

Though, she'd felt awkward buying religious artifacts when she'd grown up Christian in name only. In the end, Charity had convinced her, much like Estrella's attitude, that it couldn't hurt.

"I'm not letting anything happen to you again." Hunter pulled her close before continuing on to catch up with Tom and his crew.

"It's not up to you," Bailey said, gently. "I know you want to protect me, but you also know I have to do this and why. So, either you'll help me or you won't. I'm betting Estrella will give me permission at this point, no matter what you say. And the consequences are on me."

Hunter sighed but said nothing more about it as they chased the kids around the neighborhood, high on sugar and the energy of the night.

When they finally returned to the house, the outside lights were off and the crowds had dispersed save a few desperate onlookers, waiting for the witching hour, Bailey supposed. The police had done the trick, at least enough to make most people find better ways to spend their Halloween, and the rest to stay off the property.

When they entered the house this time, Bailey immediately felt that something had shifted. The air was thick. So thick she could hardly breathe. And the temperature was so cold their breath puffed out in front of them. At least whatever Leah and Fynn had done hadn't caused the house to explode or the walls to bleed.

Hunter had given Tom permission to sleep over at his friend Luke's house, explaining that he'd take the heat from their mother as long as he promised to be back to spend Dia De Los Muertos with the family.

"I feel better if he's out of the house," Hunter had said.

Bailey supposed he needed to protect someone, and since she wasn't letting him do it, he put his energy into saving his little brother from any potential harm.

"Has Tom seen or felt anything in the house?" Bailey asked, as Charity folded her arms around herself in a hug.

"He's always complaining someone is moving his stuff." Hunter headed straight for the kitchen. "Be right back."

The girls busied themselves with spreading out the books and protective objects they'd gathered earlier, and in a few minutes, Hunter returned with Estrella.

"I'm going up to bed now. It's been a long day." She stood beside what must've been the alter she'd spoken about earlier, now erected near the base of the stairs.

It consisted of three levels, the second packed with homemade sweets and skull-shaped candies. Orange flower petals were scattered across the black cloth, covering it and the floor below. On top was a tarnished frame containing an old picture of a couple, newly married in gown and suit, smiling adoringly at each other.

Clearly a lot of work had gone into creating this loving tribute to who Bailey guessed were Estrella's parents, Hunter's grandparents. Her heart squeezed, understanding the need to honor those departed.

"Good night," Bailey said, returning Estrella's smile and watching as the woman who, it occurred to her, looked a little older than her years, climbed the steps, hand on the railing for support. "She works too hard."

Hunter nodded. "She wants to be the perfect mother even though she has to support us. I tell her she already is, but she just laughs at me."

"What about Fynn?" Bailey asked. "Doesn't his paycheck from the mechanic help? I mean, he's always at Molly's and all over the place."

Hunter picked up one of the wooden crosses and examined it, turning it over in his hands.

"He spends it too quickly to make a dent. It's a problem."

Bailey nodded, angry at Fynn's selfishness but unwilling to make it harder on Hunter by harping on the point.

"What are you doing after graduation?" Charity asked.

"I don't know yet. I'll probably find work to help my mom." Hunter shrugged. "So, what have you discovered about our ghost?"

Bailey opened a large book and laid it in the center of the coffee table. Inside were pictures she'd printed from the library computer. She handed them to Hunter and explained as he thumbed through them.

"That first one is a good picture of Dottie." She pointed to the smiling girl, about her own age. "She disappeared one day. Didn't show up to school, and no one cared because she was an engaged girl and they assumed she'd lost interest in silly things like education." Bailey couldn't keep the sarcasm from her voice. "As you know, after they arrested her father for killing her mother a couple years later, they found that body in the attic and everyone assumed it was her. Her father even admitted to killing her when he went to prison."

Charity shivered, and Bailey didn't know if it was the cold room or the story.

"The next picture is her family before they moved in this house. The one there is her father after he was arrested. There's also a bloody crime scene photo." She waited for Hunter to catch up.

"He looks like a completely different person in the second picture," Hunter commented.

"Yeah," Bailey replied.

"He looks like he's aged about twenty years," Charity said, "but it was only four between pictures. He's all stooped and has a million lines on his face."

"Not to mention gray hair," Bailey said. "Though you can't really tell because I printed in black and white and he was blonde before."

Hunter flipped on to the next set of pictures.

"The next few are the other known victims of the house. Ingrid Blunt, Teresa Murphy, and Eileen Hampstead. All lived here at various times or were intimate with someone who did, and whose boyfriend, fiancé, or husband killed them. The fourth one is Marshall Barnett, Ingrid's fiancé, who jumped off the roof to try to and end his life, her blood still on his hands." Bailey's stomach turned, so she forced herself to focus on the facts. "None of these victims had red hair. None were named Susan."

"But," Charity was unable to contain her excitement, "we did find a few missing persons that have popped up in this town, and all about the same time. Two of their bodies were found not far from here, in what was then desert. But one, Susan Whitaker, was never found."

Hunter gaped at them.

"There's a picture of her," Bailey said. "And I sprung for the color copy on that one."

Hunter flipped to the last picture, which showed a teenage girl with a full skirt, cardigan, and bright red ponytail. She looked like she'd stepped right out of the 1950's.

"Was this the girl that saved you?" Hunter stared at the picture.

"I think so," Bailey said, choking a little on the words. "She was the one in the attic when they thought they'd found Dottie. She'd been there for at least a decade and was probably pretty decomposed."

"We think it was Richard Corvex," Charity said, "because he was the one living in the house at the time. He was never connected to the girls in the desert, but he died in a car accident near Lincoln High, a week or so after Susan was abducted."

"You think he was looking for another victim?" Hunter's voice rose. "And she was left alone in the attic to die because he couldn't get back to finish the job."

They all sat in silence for several heavy minutes.

"There's a pattern we can't deny," Bailey said. "And this was just in one afternoon. So, if we dig more, I bet we can link other men in or near the house to more disappearances, murders, and suicides."

"Like Caleb." Charity laid a hand on her friend's arm.

Bailey stiffened beneath her touch. "Don't you dare equate him to those monsters." She couldn't even look at her friend after such a suggestion.

"They may not have been monsters either," Hunter said, as careful as if he were in a cage with a wild tiger. "I think something in this house is using them to kill."

"We have to go all the way back to the beginning," Bailey said. "Back to when this place was built. Maybe even further, because that was a tragic story as well."

"He did hang himself." Charity was visibly relieved that Bailey wasn't yelling at her.

"And his wives all died." Hunter set aside the printouts. "There were like three or four of them, right? Do you think he killed them?"

"I don't know," Bailey said, pressing a finger to her bottom lip. "If I remember correctly, Caleb highlighted the one where she died of flu. So now I'm not so sure."

"Did he write anything with it?" Hunter wrinkled his forehead so much he seemed to have a unibrow.

Bailey closed her eyes, frustrated that the book was taken from her. Not only did it probably have more clues hidden inside, it was a last piece of her brother she could hold on to. She remembered finding it and how she'd run her fingers over his handwriting.

"Wait a minute." Bailey snapped her eyes open and grabbed Hunter's and Charity's arms. "I remember. One of the notes was on the eighteenth page and it was near the discussion of his wife's death. It said *check records*, and I can't believe I forgot."

"Sounds easily forgettable when you were eager to see what else was inside," Hunter's hand engulfed hers on his arm. "It's such a benign statement."

"Except that now we know what he meant." Charity was already on her phone, Googling.

"He didn't think it was likely she died from flu," Bailey said, "and I don't either. Did you find anything, Charity? Too bad the library's closed."

"Yeah, I can't check records from here, but I looked up the name Travis Beckham. Hold on, I'm reading his bio on Wiki."

"Well, that's reliable," Hunter muttered. "I mean, maybe it was the same thing using him. Maybe this was an Indian burial ground or something. Maybe it was a demon hanging around and wanting kill and ruin as many as possible. Maybe—"

"Maybe it's him," Charity said, turning her phone over to flash an old-fashioned photograph at the others. A man stood holding the lapels of a late-1800's-style suitcoat. He wore a hat and had long bushy sideburns and deep shadows underneath dark eyes.

"Mr. Muttonchops?" Hunter asked with a grin.

Bailey elbowed him. "Is that Beckham?"

Charity nodded. "No one ever talks about what he did before he built this house, other than his struggle to make it from a runaway to a farmhand, et cetera. There was a quick mention that his bad luck started early in life when his mother abandoned him and his sister."

"Abandonment issues?" Bailey asked.

"Well, maybe. Or maybe he killed her. There was never another record of her, according to this. Then again, it's not reliable. Hunter's right there."

"What about the sister?" Hunter asked. "What happened to her?"

Charity's thumbs moved expertly over the face of the phone as she sucked in her bottom lip in concentration. When she stopped, her eyes grew wide.

"Constance Beckham. She joined the local brothel."

"Nice," Bailey said. "Then what?"

"Hold on." Again, Charity's thumbs raced across the phone. "I looked up deaths and the brothel name. It said many of the soiled doves ended up dying of syphilis, and that several were found murdered in their beds." Charity set down the phone. "No one seemed to care about them. I don't think it even made more than a mention in the papers."

"What if they were murdered by the same guy?" Bailey said. "Maybe one was his sister and he liked killing girls before the house was built."

"I think we're going a little too far on conjecture," Hunter said and sat back against the cushions. "These things could've simply happened at the same time."

"Maybe," Bailey agreed, but inside something assured her she was right.

Call it a sixth sense, or maybe the face in the picture felt like the shadow man that kept attacking her.

"Did he smoke?" she asked Charity.

Charity checked her phone. "Cigars. Imported expensive ones once he could afford them."

"That's not a coincidence," Bailey said, turning toward Hunter. "You've smelled it, too, haven't you? The air reeked of it before he attacked me on the stairs."

"Lots of men smoked back then," he said, leaning forward again and crisscrossing his fingers together. "And even if his ghost is here, it might not be the evil one."

"It's not a demon, it's a man. I've seen him. Or at least, part of him. And I've felt him." Bailey shuddered at the memory of the weight on her at the bottom of the steps. "It's a man that hates girls, and right now he hates me."

Hunter's face blanched, and Bailey was sure he was tempted to try and throw her out of the house for her own good, but he stayed silent.

Inside, she was shaking. This thing had murdered or caused the murder of at least a dozen women, probably many more, and it was… *playing* with her. That was the word. Yes, it had tried to kill her when she was in the attic, but that was a burst of momentary anger because she was about to find something. She definitely got the sense that this thing liked to torture its victims. Just look at poor Susan, shackled in the attic. It seemed that the later victims were kept alive longer, like he'd grown more confident and needed more cruelty to satisfy his murderous urges.

Bailey shivered and grabbed a throw pillow to hug over herself as she leaned back into the sofa. What if she was the next intended victim? That meant they needed to figure out how to get rid of it before it claimed her.

Bailey stood and tossed the pillow aside. "We need to get into the attic."

CHAPTER 17

"Actually, I'd like to go to the cemetery." Charity stood too and scanned her phone.

"What?" Bailey was sufficiently thrown off by her friend's comment that she sat back down on the edge of the sofa.

"I want to see if we can find the graves of the victims and see if there are any date connections. Or maybe even find Constance or the other soiled doves. I like that term for them. It may help our investigation, and it could also help put their souls to rest. According to this website, sometimes it just takes acknowledging them."

"Sounds good to me," Hunter said, standing as well.

Bailey gaped at her friends. "But the trunk. That has to be important."

Hunter offered her a hand up and pulled her close, draping an arm over her shoulder. "The more information we have before we face this thing again, the better."

He was the voice of reason, quietly persuading her in her ear. It was maddening to be so close to what she knew had to be an answer and not be able to reach it because of an invisible force.

"Let's go," Bailey said. "Charity, bring all the supplies. I'm going to stop at home really quick also." She headed toward the door.

The sooner they had all the intel the others felt necessary, the sooner she could get back to the trunk in the attic.

"What do you need at home?" Hunter asked.

"Chocolate." Bailey shrugged and led the way outside.

By the time they reached the cemetery, it was close to three in the morning, a time that Bailey had learned, through her binging of ghost shows, was the beginning of the true witching hour.

She took the last bite of a Snickers Mini and tossed the wrapper in the trash near the gate. The rolling hills of Shadow Springs Cemetery were alive on Halloween night. Pockets of people, mostly their own ages, had settled into various areas among the dead. Bursts of occasional laughter pierced the blanket of night, and the herbal scent of marijuana was easy to detect.

Charity led the way to the older part of the grounds, where the gravestones stood erect, sometimes cracked and broken or overgrown. These were from the times before people started setting the stones flat for fear of earthquake damage. Here, the graves were closer together and unevenly laid.

Hunter took her hand in his when they spotted a pocket of hooded figures grouped around a huge stone angel, wings spread and kneeling over a sarcophagus.

Charity stopped. "Are those the people that were in front of the house earlier?" she whispered.

"I think so." Bailey was unsure whether they posed any threat or were just weirdos.

She recalled the Ouija board they'd left behind and the warning it had given.

Shivering, she cleared her throat and called out, "I called Sergeant Harper. Thought I'd give you all a warning this time."

"Oh man," the closest of the figures replied, removing his hood to reveal a twenty-something-year-old guy with a close-shaved head and several piercings. "What'd we do to you?"

"You invaded my property," Hunter said, stepping in front of them. "And now you're messing with my ancestor's grave."

"You're related to Eugenia Beckham?" the guy said doubtfully as the others lowered their hoods one by one.

Bailey could see they each held another black candle.

"So?" Hunter asked, clearly as shocked as Bailey felt.

That was exactly where they needed to start their investigation, with Travis Beckham's first wife, who supposedly died of flu.

The guy shrugged and glanced back at his crew. "It's just that she had no kids. So... how are you related?"

"Her cousin, Jeremy Sothstand, is his great grandfather," Charity said.

Thank goodness for her thoroughness in research.

The group of figures huddled together momentarily, speaking quickly in hushed voices.

"Um." The man faced them again. "If you could call off the sheriff, we were just wondering if we could maybe ask you a few questions. I mean, maybe you can set some things straight for us." He shifted awkwardly on his feet.

Bailey exchanged looks with her own group. These people weren't scary—weird for sure—but scary, not so much. *Maybe they have a stake in this, too*. She motioned for the others to huddle together so they could talk.

"They might have more information," she whispered.

"What happens when they figure out we're lying?" Charity said. "I mean, I remembered the name of her relative. I don't know any more than that."

"I think we should risk it," Bailey said. "I can always say I'll call Sergeant Harper." She turned back to the group. "Fine. I'll text him right now." She typed at her phone, pretending to text the policeman.

"Cool." The man leading the group seemed to relax a little, and even half-smiled. "I'm Paul, by the way."

"Bailey, Hunter, and Charity," Bailey said, reaching out a hand to shake his.

They joined the group around the sarcophagus of Eugenia, and someone offered them some hot cocoa from a Thermos as Paul explained that they were a group of pagans, self-described, that felt their purpose was to uncover the secrets of the Gallows House. Apparently, they believed there was a portal to another dimension in the house somewhere, created by Beckham.

"Why?" Hunter furrowed his brows.

It was a stretch, even for Bailey's imagination.

Paul took a gulp of cocoa, which Bailey wasn't convinced was pure chocolate.

"He dabbled in the Black Arts."

Charity gasped. "He practiced black magic?"

"Oh, yeah," Paul said. "Totally. Take a look at our bible."

He motioned for one of the women in the back of the group, who rummaged through their things to produce a binder full of old pictures and letters, each protected beneath a sheet of plastic. The top was black and had white calligraphy letters that read BIBLE.

Hunter coughed as Bailey took the book and began to thumb through, the others looking over her shoulder. She recognized the man featured in the photos to be the builder of the house, by his muttonchops. He looked like a werewolf to Bailey. He stood posing with a hunting rifle in one hand, sleeves rolled up and the carcass of a deer underfoot.

"There, see?" Paul stopped her from flipping and pointed to the picture. "We blew it up."

He flipped it so they could see a large image of the man's right side, with the rifle from the previous photo. It was beyond grainy, but it was still possible to make out the pentagram tattooed on his forearm. Bailey had to admit, it was weird, but she wasn't convinced that it meant what they assumed.

Paul flipped ahead and handed the book back to her.

"Here he is with the blueprints for the house," he said and pointed to the tiny blurry section of ground beneath what Bailey assumed to be where the willow stood.

It was a small pentagram design that one of them had gone over with a marker.

"I don't understand," Bailey said.

"We think he had the remains of his mother buried there. It's very powerful magic because she was well known to be a witch, by the community of the time. The only reason they didn't suspect him was because she supposedly abandoned him as a child."

"Supposedly?" Bailey asked.

"She dropped off the face of the earth, but his sister was considered mad because she used to say she'd seen her fall out of the window and then disappear like a witch."

"I'm surprised people didn't believe her." Charity perched on top of another gravestone. "The way people thought of witches back then."

Paul nodded like she really got it. "Exactly. But he told everyone she was crazy. Said he'd seen his mother leave through the front door. We think he killed her to absorb her power and hid the body before his sister could get to it. No one really knows."

"That's a big leap," Hunter said. "And that's a pretty old picture. There's no way to know for sure that's even a pentagram."

"Maybe." Paul shrugged. "But there's more, starting with your cousin here. Did you know that there were no other flu victims that year? A rarity for sure."

"Unlucky for her," Bailey said.

"According to the records, she languished for months, keeping to her rooms, where she would only see her doting husband. Then when she finally died, he wouldn't let anyone near the body, for fear they'd contract the malady."

"So, no one actually ever saw the body?" Bailey asked. "Didn't a doctor declare her dead or something?"

"He and the town doctor were good friends," Paul said, as though closing the case. "And by that time, he was wealthy enough to pay off a man, who by all accounts, was always well-dressed and apt to toss his wealth around like nothing."

"So, he had the doctor in his pocket," Charity said. "Certainly helpful if you're a serial killer."

"Bingo." Paul was practically jumping up and down. "His other wives died in accidents that left their bodies broken and bruised. But what if it *wasn't* from the accidents? And did you know he had the others cremated and kept on the property?"

"But why?" Bailey asked.

"For various spells," Paul answered. "It all makes sense."

"This is all a little farfetched for me," Hunter said, stuffing his hands in his pockets and leaning back against the sarcophagus.

"Do you think," Bailey said, "he would've had the power to hang around after death? And maybe manipulate people who were still alive?"

Paul shrugged. "Sure. He could've made a deal with the devil, for all I know."

Hunter snorted at that, but goosebumps formed on Bailey's skin. The more she heard, the surer she was that Beckham was the one responsible for everything.

"Our turn," Paul said. "So, what did the family say about Eugenia's death?"

Someone from the back shuffled forward with a notepad and pen.

Hunter seemed confused and Bailey kicked him a little.

"Oh. They believed the story about the flu. They saw Beckham as a devoted husband."

"So, the funeral was here?" Disappointment rang in Paul's voice.

"Yeah, but it wasn't open casket," Hunter added, sounding more confident the further he went with the story. "That doesn't prove anything, though."

"This could be empty," Paul said. "That would prove something."

"If your plan is to exhume a grave." Charity hopped down off the stone. "I doubt that thing is going to open."

"We have ways. But since it's your relative, if you give us permission..." he looked at Hunter, hopefully.

"I can't give you that," Hunter said quickly. "Let her rest."

"What if she isn't in there and she isn't at rest at all?" Bailey stared at the angel over the elaborate grave. "I think we should open it."

"What?" Hunter grabbed her by the arms and turned her to look him in the eyes.

"Excuse us a second," she said to Paul, and led Hunter off to the side, by the hand. "We have to help her rest if she isn't in there."

"What if she's perfectly comfortable and we disturb her?" he hissed.

"She's not in there," Bailey said with certainty.

Hunter pressed her face between his hands and searched her eyes.

"How can you be sure? What if you want to believe this guy's story so you have an explanation? Bailey, you can't be serious."

"I am. Please, just listen." She fidgeted and stared up at him. "He was collecting them. The women he killed. You know how serial killers keep trophies? I think he was keeping their bodies, and maybe more."

"More?"

Bailey was thinking of Dottie and Susan's ghosts and the way they tried to save her and interfere with him. Dottie's desperate words. *Find me.*

"We have to find them and remove them to free them from him." Bailey was never surer of anything in her life. "Do you trust me?"

Hunter stared into her eyes for long time, clearly battling over something in his mind. Finally, he let out a long breath and released her face to once again stuff his hands in his pockets.

"Okay," he said in a loud voice that carried above the gravestones. "Let's do this thing."

CHAPTER 18

This time last year Bailey, would never have pictured herself in a graveyard at 3:30 a.m. on Halloween, breaking into a sarcophagus. But nothing had been the same since her brother's death, and she promised herself she'd no longer be surprised by anything.

"Push," Paul said, and everyone shoved with all their might, causing a horrible grinding sound that Bailey was sure would attract the police.

Paul and his friends had brought along large shovels and various other tools that they'd used to pry into the seam where the two-ton lid met the sides of the coffin. Once they'd managed to slide it a good inch, the smell of stale air had escaped, along with a number of creepy crawly things that Bailey would rather forget.

As they heaved again with all their strength, Bailey's heart beat faster because the smell of rot had been conspicuously absent. And on the fifth shove, the stone finally slid aside enough to see inside.

Collectively, they held their breath as sixteen heads peered over the side, where a layer of dirt, dust, and cobwebs highlighted the enormous empty space. Murmurs of congratulations sounded all around, and Bailey collapsed back against Hunter, relieved and elated at the same time, because it meant she was right, and she knew what she was supposed to do. Still, she didn't know how it connected to Caleb. Because she couldn't and wouldn't accept that he'd been manipulated by this monster of a man's spirit.

"Now what?" Charity asked, interrupting the celebrations.

"We put it back," Paul said, and everyone groaned.

And so, Bailey returned to her house on the first day of November, at five in the morning, exhausted physically and mentally, and ready for a good long sleep. It was only three hours later, however, that her father shook her awake.

"What?" Bailey moaned, batting at her father's offending hands.

"Bailey, wake up. Are you okay?"

Bailey rubbed her eyes and yawned, sitting up in bed. What planet was her father from? He was waking her up to see if she was okay?

"Yeah, I'm fine. Just sleeping. Why?" She yawned again as her father's drawn face came into focus.

"Thank God. I'm sorry to wake you, but I can't lose you, too." Her father folded her into a too-tight hug, rocking her like a baby.

Bailey's pulse zoomed into overdrive as she returned the embrace. Something had really shaken him. But what?

"Dad? What's happening?" she asked, trying to pry herself away enough to see his face.

"Hopefully, nothing. Hopefully I'm just overreacting. It's Leah Tucker, from your school. She's in your grade."

"Yeah, I know Leah. What happened?" Bailey's panic grew as her father's distress continued.

"She's missing. She never came home last night. Her parents said she was going out with friends."

A cold feeling started in Bailey's stomach and slithered out into her limbs. Her mind buzzed like a radio not tuned into a station. *Leah, gone?*

Bailey was one of the friends she was supposed to be with. It was Bailey's fault she'd gone out with Fynn instead of sticking with them. She'd shut down the homework group for the night, so she was partially to blame.

"I'm so sorry, Bailey. I should've been more sensitive. I didn't realize you knew her so well."

Bailey slowly came back to reality, realizing tears had splashed down onto her quilt.

"Was she the type of girl to hang with a bad crowd? Did she drink? Maybe she's okay and just hungover?"

"Dad." Bailey backed up against the headboard.

Was her father victim-blaming? What the hell?

"I'm just saying, maybe it's not as bad as we're thinking."

Bailey nodded, numb, as she thought about the last time she'd seen Leah, curled around Fynn, insisting on playing with the Ouija board. And Fynn. What about him? Had he started drinking? Was he somehow under the influence of Beckham? Oh, God. She had to tell Hunter. And what about Estrella?

"I have to go," she said, aware that she sounded way too calm.

She slipped off the bed and rummaged for some clothes. She needed a shower bigtime. She had been too tired when she'd gotten home, and she was vaguely aware of the layer of grime that still covered her body from the graveyard.

"What did you do last night?" her father asked.

"We hung out in town. Nothing big."

"Then where are you going now?" her father demanded, standing. "I want you to stay here with me today. It's Sunday and I need to know where you are."

"I can't." Bailey faced her dad, aware of her disheveled appearance and the twigs probably still tangled in her hair. "I promised Hunter I'd finish the report. And Charity."

"They can come here, then."

She nodded reluctantly and snatched up her phone to bring in the bathroom with her. Why'd he have to be so damn reasonable?

She texted Charity and Hunter, and told Charity to go get him at the house on the way over in case her messages still weren't getting through. They should meet at Bailey's house in an hour, and she was sorry Hunter had to find out this way, but that he should figure out what happened to Fynn last night.

Bailey's mind worked on overdrive as she undressed and showered. Leah had no clue what she had gotten herself into. Bailey should've been honest and told her everything. She'd been so afraid of letting people in. And why? Because at some level she was scared she was wrong. Wrong about her brother choosing to take his life and leave her behind. She couldn't let herself believe it. Not when she'd always thought of Caleb as her hero who could do no wrong. She'd trusted him completely, expected him to be the strong one. How could she have been so wrong? How could someone she gave her heart and trust to so freely find it so easy to leave her behind without so much as a note?

The hot water slid over her back as she leaned against the contrast of the cool tile wall. Her tears mixed with the flowing stream.

"Why won't you even visit me?" she whispered into the ether.

It's what she'd wanted all along, because if he was still around in some form, then he hadn't really left her behind. It was what she'd assumed the day she found his book, that Caleb was there, communicating with her and helping her to solve the mystery of his death. That he *had* thought of her before dying but couldn't stop it from happening despite that. That he was, still there for her even in death.

"It wasn't you, was it?" she asked, in a small voice, between sobs. "It was Dottie, I think, or one of the women from the house. I don't know how I know, but I feel it's true. I would've known if it was you."

Bailey slid down the wall to sit in the tub as the water washed over her. But it couldn't wash away the pain. She stayed there a long time, hugging her knees and sobbing into them, before turning the knobs and forcing herself to get ready for her friends' arrival.

"Why did you leave me?" she asked, wiping at the steam in the mirror as she had the day she spotted Dottie behind her.

Today there was no one, and she hadn't expected them either. Even on this, the Day of the Dead, either Caleb was unable or unwilling to reach her, and she had to accept that, as hard as it was.

Head aching and throat thick, Bailey put herself together as best she could, choosing to wear grey jeans and a black tank beneath Caleb's black and green plaid shirt, with her black and white checked high-tops, as they were the closest she had to somber colors. She felt like she was really mourning her brother for the first time. For the first time, she was acknowledging the possibility that he wasn't the person she always thought he was. That he was human and fallible, and that opening herself up to trusting others might be a fatal flaw in her personality. Her Achilles heel, destined to be her downfall, at least emotionally.

"I made you and your friends some cinnamon rolls for breakfast," her father said, by way of greeting.

She hadn't even noticed him she was so deep in thought and self-pity.

"And there's a fresh pot of coffee on. Do they drink coffee?" He twisted his fingers by the kitchen island, eyes bloodshot.

"That's great, Dad. Thanks."

"It's the least I can do," he continued, squeezing readymade frosting on the cinnamon buns. Though it smelled delicious, it wasn't a match for Estrella's homemade sweetbread, nor did Bailey feel much like eating, especially anything else that was sweet.

"You don't need to do anything special," Bailey said, as the doorbell rang. "I mean, it's scary about Leah, but there's nothing you can do."

"Actually, there is. And it isn't about Leah."

She reached for the handle, two shadows, one tall and one short, on the other side of the glass.

"What?" She turned back to her father.

"We have an appointment for the two of us to see a grief counselor, tomorrow morning. There won't be much real instruction in school tomorrow anyway, so I decided it was a good time."

"But—"

Bailey started to protest, not wanting any time taken from her investigation, but quickly realized it was important for both of them. They'd been so good at pretending nothing was wrong since Mom left, that they'd forgotten to be a family. Maybe Leah's disappearance had kick-started more than her own grief.

"Okay," she said.

Bailey opened the door, letting Charity and Hunter inside, the latter looking so high-strung she was afraid he might hit the ceiling if she touched him.

They politely accepted breakfast from her father, who went up to his room to give them privacy, at Bailey's request. Then they stared down at their untouched cinnamon rolls.

Hunter finally broke the silence. "He's gone. At least, he's not home."

"Fynn?" Bailey asked. "So maybe they just went somewhere together?"

Hunter looked at her, pain written on his beautiful face.

Bailey sighed deeply. "I assume you texted him?"

"And called. Goes straight to voicemail. And for the record, I got your texts this morning."

Bailey nodded, stomach twisting in knots as she remembered the Fynn from that night in the police car.

"If it's Beckham controlling him," Charity said, stirring sugar in her coffee, "we need to stop him before he does something to Leah."

"He wouldn't hurt her," Hunter said, slamming his fist down on the table, which made all their coffees slosh dangerously near the edge of the cups.

"Not of his own volition," Bailey said. "But it won't matter to the police. Not when they've seen the way he acted with Sam that night."

"That and his family history." Hunter let his head collapse on top of his folded arms in defeat, making Bailey even more determined.

"Come on. We're taking a drive to LA." She jumped up and started rummaging for her father's keys.

"Wait. What's in LA?" Charity asked. "Do you think that's where they are?"

"No. But Amber is, and she has answers to some of my questions. She might be able to help Leah."

"Won't your dad be mad?" Charity asked, as Bailey opened the door to usher them out.

"He'll get over it. I don't have time to argue with him. Every minute we waste is another minute Leah could be hurt."

Hunter rose from the table and followed her without another word.

"Maybe you should stay here, Charity. Try to calm my dad down and tell him we're at the library or something. Then try to find out what you can about places they may have gone last night."

"Will do," Charity said, looking relieved, as Bailey had figured. She'd be in her element doing research.

Bailey threw the car into reverse and backed out as Hunter looked up directions on his phone. On the hour-and-a-half drive through LA traffic, they discussed what they'd uncovered so far. Keeping to the facts helped both of them stay focused and sane.

"Why is this happening?" Hunter fiddled with the radio knobs after he'd located Amber's address near UCLA.

"I don't know." Bailey tightened her grip on the wheel. "We're going to save them, though. Both of them." She moved one hand to rest on his knee.

She wouldn't let him lose a brother the way she had.

Amber's apartment sat across from a pretty urban park near UCLA. A sudden thought occurred to Bailey as they raced up the steps to the correct number. What if she wasn't there? After all their effort, there was no guarantee she'd be home anytime soon.

Her fears were unfounded, because within a minute the door opened and Amber's familiar heart-shaped face gaped at her from the other side, azure eyes wide and frightened.

"Can we come in?" Bailey asked.

She thought she would feel anger being here with Amber, who'd been such a fixture in their home, always in physical contact with Caleb, like she couldn't bear to be separated from him. And then she left before he was even laid to rest. But Bailey only felt sorrow.

"You're wearing the shirt I bought him last Christmas," Amber said. "Less than a month before it happened."

She watched Bailey and Hunter claim their seats on the futon that doubled as a sofa in the living area of the tiny apartment that should've been her brother's. A shadow seemed to cross her face, revealing a moment of sorrow and pain, that disappeared as quickly as it came.

Bailey pulled the green and black plaid shirt around herself. She hadn't realized Amber had given Caleb this one.

Amber hugged herself before rummaging in the refrigerator.

"This is Hunter," Bailey said, introducing him as she accepted a can of soda from Amber. "I'm going to go ahead and cut to the chase. He's living in the Gallows House, with his family. They're good people, but his brother is acting strange. You said," Bailey paused, setting the unopened can down on the crate acting as a side table then took a breath to steady herself. "You said Caleb attacked you that night. You ran, even though I believe you loved him, and I need to know why."

The three of them sat silent for a few moments as Amber played with the end of her braid, eyes swimming with tears.

"I knew you'd ask someday," she finally said. "I just didn't know how to tell you what happened. I never told anyone the whole story because after the police dismissed it, I knew no one would ever believe me. *I* wouldn't have if I hadn't been there."

"We'll believe you," Hunter said in his quiet, calm voice. "Please. There are lives at stake. My brother's life."

Amber crossed her legs, then uncrossed them. "There's nothing you can do. That's the first thing you have to understand. There's no magic answer or way to solve the puzzle that Caleb imagined was there."

"You mean, about the house?" Bailey asked.

"Yes." Amber nodded, solemnly. "I watched him lose himself in it. For our whole senior year, until the day I lost him. It started with that stupid assignment."

"He'd been obsessed with the house a lot longer than that." Bailey lowered her gaze. "He used to tell me stories about it when I was little. Over and over."

Amber shrugged. "I guess he sensed whatever was there. Maybe it was using him long before we ever went there."

"What happened that night?" Bailey asked.

A familiar layer of bricks lay at the bottom of her stomach.

"We'd gone to the house to break in through the back window, but the door was already wide open."

Bailey pictured the kitchen door creaking open for her that day. This time, she doubted it was Dottie who'd let them in.

"I had a bad feeling about it and I begged him to reconsider, but he told me he had to. He said I could go home if I wanted, and I should've listened." Amber hung her head. "Instead, I held his hand as tight as I could and followed him inside as he led the way with his flashlight. Inside, everything felt frozen in time, dusty and deserted. No matter what room we went in, I never felt alone. It was like there were always eyes on me, watching."

"Why didn't you run?" Bailey asked.

"Caleb convinced me there was nothing to be afraid of. I thought he could protect me. But I didn't know he couldn't protect himself."

"Did Caleb attack you?" Bailey asked.

"Yes," Amber said, her voice filled with pain. "But I... I don't think it was Caleb anymore. After we went upstairs, he started to change. He was muttering to himself like he was arguing with someone. He kept pulling away and wouldn't let me near him, and then..."

"What?"

Amber pulled her knees up in the chair with her, wrapping her arms around them.

"He started getting, you know... flirty. He wanted to make-out, like it was all a plan to get me alone in a haunted house. But I knew it didn't make sense. It wasn't like him, and it didn't feel right when he was kissing me. Look, I know he was your brother, and this is hard to talk about, so if you don't want to hear it—"

"Tell me," Bailey said.

"Okay. Well, he started getting forceful, holding me down on the bed and... biting me. I tried to pull away, but he held me harder, hurt my wrists." Amber's voice shook as she described the attack. "He laughed, but it wasn't his laugh. It was someone else's. I called him out on it, and his eyes—they turned black. I mean all of them, the whites, the irises, everything. It was the most scared I'd ever been."

Visions of Fynn in the back of the police car flashed through Bailey's mind, and how his eyes seemed to change.

"How'd you get away?" Hunter asked.

"I didn't. Not yet," The panic of the moment appeared in Amber's voice. "I told him my parents knew where we were. I screamed and fought, and he told me that he was going to put me where no one would ever find me, and I'd be his to do with whatever he wanted, forever."

Amber cried quietly into her knees for a while as Bailey looked at Hunter, a million thoughts flying through her mind.

"He... he said he'd make me beg." Amber cried into her lap.

But Bailey heard her loud and clear, and once again visions of Fynn bragging about forcing her to say *please* flashed through her mind.

"You did get away, right?" Bailey was ashamed for having forced this out of Amber.

That wasn't her brother talking. She was starting to understand why Amber couldn't face them at the funeral.

Amber raised her head, eyes red and face streaked with tears. "After about twenty minutes of hell that I won't go into, I managed to hit him in the jaw with my foot. At this point, he had my hands tied to the bedpost, with my shirt." Amber averted her gaze. "When I struck him, I think Caleb came out again and he untied me, yelling at me to run and get the hell out."

"Then what did you do?" Bailey was horrified.

"I ran and didn't look back. That night, he texted me one last time." She broke down into sobs.

Bailey waited, unsure if she should try to comfort her or not.

"What did it say?" She was at war with her sense of pity and her sense of entitlement.

"It said, I'm sorry." Amber wailed. "And it was sent just before three AM."

"Right before he pulled the trigger." Bailey felt like the bricks were trying to come up through her throat.

"I didn't want to go to the funeral because I was scared that the person in the casket wouldn't be Caleb. And I couldn't take that,

Bailey. I'm sorry. I'm so sorry. And I tried to make a report to the police, but they kept telling my parents I was in shock. They wouldn't listen." Amber held out her hands, begging for forgiveness.

"It *was* him." Bailey stood, with Hunter at her back. "In the casket, that was him. I think he was fighting it and it was the only way he could win the battle. He loved you so much that he died so you'd be safe."

Amber gawked at her through her tears, then began to cry harder.

Hunter put a hand on Bailey's shoulder and squeezed. "It wasn't your fault," he said to Amber. "It was the evil in the house, and it sounds like Caleb was a strong guy to hold off the evil like that. I don't think just anyone could've done that. Thank you for telling us what happened. I know it was painful, but even details you don't think were important could make the difference for my brother."

Bailey swallowed back her tears, glad that Hunter was with her and could say what needed to be said, the right way.

"We need to know something else, though," he said, hesitantly. "We need to know where you were when the attack happened, and if he said anything about where he was going to keep you when he said he'd have you forever. Anything you tell us could help us save multiple lives."

"What's this about?" Amber stood and hugged herself. "We were upstairs, in a bedroom of some sort. It had thick red curtains and the bed had high posts."

"There's a girl missing," Bailey said. "Last we saw her, she was in the house last night, with Hunter's brother."

"You said your brother was acting weird?" Amber asked, stepping forward, suddenly frantic. She peered over their shoulders at the door like he may burst through at any moment. "He's probably been possessed by whatever got into Caleb. You need to go. I can't take any more of this in my life. I'm sorry."

"You can help us save her, and you don't have to go anywhere near the house," Bailey begged, as Hunter headed straight for the door. "Was there anything else you can tell us about where he may've taken her? You're the only one I know of that's ever survived."

"No. There was nothing else. I told you everything. Now get out and don't come back. That part of my life is over. I'm sorry about Caleb, Bailey. I really am."

Bailey swallowed back the rest of her pleas and tugged the shirt from off her shoulders. She handed it to Amber, who accepted it, staring down at it in her hands like a lost child, then held it to her face and began to sob once again.

CHAPTER 19

Bailey let herself out, along with Hunter, into what had turned into a cold November morning. The winds had picked up, and leaves and twigs blew around their feet, pelting their ankles like tiny attackers. A single tear wove down Bailey's cheek. A single tear that carried with it sorrow and helplessness for Caleb, Amber, Fynn, and Leah, and for all the people this monster had hurt throughout the years.

"I'm going to stop him from hurting any more people," Bailey said, "and I'm going to release all those souls."

Hunter's hand found hers and together they walked in silence, back to the car.

"It's Fynn's bedroom," Hunter said, after an hour on the road.

"What?" Bailey was shaken out of her swirling thoughts.

"The room Amber described being attacked in, with the red curtains. It's where Fynn sleeps."

"We should check there first," Bailey said. "We're going straight there, because if I go home there's a good chance my father won't let me leave the house until I'm twenty-one."

When they arrived, there was a crowd pressing in on the house, as usual. Bailey could pick out familiar faces this time. Worse, they had the sense of an angry mob more than curious onlookers. It didn't help that there was a police car parked in front.

The group parted to let the car through, and they rushed, hand-in-hand, to the front door, which opened for them. Tom was on the other side, looking green. Bailey wrapped him in a hug the second she saw him and surveyed the room. Estrella sat on the couch with a worn tissue in her hands. Sergeant Harper sat with her, pale and drawn, eyes full of concern. It was a face Bailey remembered all too well from her own house, after Caleb's death. She must've blocked out a lot of the details of that day. But seeing him like this made it all come rushing back.

"What's going on?" Hunter asked, looking around the room, from one person to another. "Where's Fynn?"

"I was going to ask you the same question," Sergeant Harper said, trying to sound easy-going in a way that made the comment stand out as a threat even more.

"He and the devil girl didn't come back last night." Estrella's voice shook with worry. "We can't reach him on his phone."

"Devil girl?" Harper asked.

"That was the costume she was wearing," Bailey let Tom go to move into the room, careful to act like she didn't know too much. "They're both missing?"

"Leah is a minor," Harper said, cautiously. "So, it doesn't look good that they disappeared together."

"They found his truck," Estrella said, through tears. "Abandoned on the side of the road."

"Where?" Bailey and Hunter asked.

"Near the cemetery," Harper said. "We have men searching the area."

"And they won't give us the truck back," Estrella said, accusation in her voice.

"We have to keep it as evidence," Harper said to Hunter, trying to reason with the least hysterical member of the family.

"Evidence?" Hunter said. "That means you think there's been a crime."

"At the very least, like I said, there's the issue of Leah being a minor." Harper stood. "Her parents are hysterical right now, understandably. I guess they didn't know she was going out with Fynn. With this being a small town and all, well, they've heard about the incident the other night and they're pretty upset. If we find them well and good, though, there's a decent chance they'll calm down and won't press charges."

"I'll press charges against them for leading my boy astray." Estrella stood also, waving her tissue at the officer.

"Mama." Hunter rushed over to pull her to his side. "This is very hard on her, Officer. Please understand."

"And the *incident* the other night?" Estrella took a fistful of Hunter's shirt. "How could you keep this from me, *mijo*?"

Hunter's face fell and his carefully held façade of calm broke in two. Bailey would've done anything to change what they were going through. She remembered all too well the feeling of betrayal when Amber told them Caleb had attacked her prior to his suicide.

"Innocent until proven guilty." Bailey said, taking the Sargent's arm and leading him to the door. "Let them know the moment you find anything. I'm sure you have places to search besides the cemetery."

"Come, Mama," Hunter said, as Bailey closed and locked the door behind Sergeant Harper. "I'll make you some tea."

"Tom, how about you show me Fynn's room?" Bailey motioned for the boy to lead the way up the steps. "Maybe there'll be a clue as to where he may've gone."

With a nod, Tom led the way upstairs and down the hall, to a door just like all the others. Out of either habit or courtesy, he knocked and then opened it for Bailey.

"I'm going to be in my room." He kept his head down, clearly unable to look at the interior.

Bailey understood. She gave him a quick hug and promised to let him know if she found anything that clued them in to his whereabouts.

The air inside the room was charged with something like static electricity, but still not familiar enough to name. The majority of the room was taken up by the immense king-sized four poster and a dresser across the way. The window was covered in the thick burgundy curtains trimmed in gold that blocked out any natural light, and Bailey shivered, recalling Amber's story and seeing the room through her eyes.

Fynn's clothes were all over and the bed wasn't made, probably from the day before. Bailey let out a sigh. At least she hadn't found Leah bound to the bed, though she didn't know what she expected. Surely someone would have at least looked for Fynn here already.

Since she was there, she decided to do a more thorough search, beginning under the bed and ending with the dresser drawers. It was when she shut the last one that she noticed the worn corner of a brown book poking out from a pile of papers on the dresser. With trembling fingers, she pulled the book from the pile, thumbing through the pages punctuated with yellow highlighter and Caleb's familiar scrawl. Fury rose inside her, bubbling up from the pit of her stomach. Clutching the book, she retreated from the room and shut the door behind her.

She retreated to Hunter's bedroom to wait, and climbed up on his own giant bed, the only place in this godforsaken house that had good memories not yet ruined by the evil of a single man from over a century ago.

"Come on, Caleb. You knew it was him, didn't you? You figured this out and you were looking for clues, too, when you came here with Amber. Somehow, Beckham got inside you, and when you deprived him of your body, he decided to take over Fynn's."

It felt good to talk to Caleb out loud, like she used to in his room. She missed being able to pull his shirt around her, so she compensated by using Hunter's soft duvet as she flipped through the book.

"What am I missing that you figured out? There has to be something in here, or he wouldn't have bothered taking it."

Some of his comments now made sense in the context of what they'd found out. Things like comments in the histories. The killers that showed no problems until they moved into the house. Bailey stopped going in order and closed the book so that the spine sat in her lap.

She closed her eyes. "Dottie, if you're here, I need a helping hand again. Help me find what I need."

Dropping the front and back at the same time, the book fell open to roughly a center page with no writing or highlighting on it. Bailey sighed, wondering where all the ghosts had gone when, a cold wind swept through the room, much like it had when she'd found the book the first time. Or rather, when the book had found her. She smiled as the pages began to flutter and flip backward, toward the front. When the wind died and the book settled, page thirteen stared up at her. The paragraph highlighted was the introduction to Beckham and his whirlwind romance with wife number one, for whom he built the house as a wedding gift.

Did he know yet? Read Caleb's scribble in the margin. *Check blueprint originals.*

Blueprint originals? Know what? Bailey closed the book, frustrated, but forced herself to focus. Whirlwind romance. Maybe he didn't know he was going to end up killing his wife? Maybe the original blueprints…

"Didn't include something he added later, when he realized he'd be needing it to hide his wives' bodies," Bailey said out loud.

The room's temperature dropped drastically and the overhead light dimmed, then went out for a few seconds.

"I wish I could actually talk to you," Bailey said to the room at large. "How many of you are still trapped here?"

The drapes on Hunter's windows began to blow inward despite the glass sitting in place, and the heavy scent of rose perfume permeated the air. A white mist gathered along the floor, pooling in swirls that swallowed the hardwood floor and the legs of Hunter's wooden desk chair. Bailey watched in wonder as tendrils of mist climbed the edge of the bed, reaching toward each other in the spot opposite her, until they formed the outline of what looked like a woman with long flowing hair. The image wavered, along with the ever-moving mist as it raised two ghostly hands, and the number thirteen formed for a moment. By the time Bailey released her next breath, it was gone, and the words *save us* echoed inside her mind.

"I'm trying," she said, desperation and frustration threatening to consume her. Is this what Caleb had realized? Is this why he was so obsessed?

The door to the room swung open, making Bailey jolt upright as the remaining mist disintegrated into nothing, leaving only the memory behind, late afternoon sunlight slipping in through the cracks in the curtains and highlighting bits of floating dust over the wood floor.

"Sorry it took me so long," Hunter said, joining her to sit on the edge of the bed where he pulled his long fingers back through his mess of hair. "Mama is pretty upset. I told her we'd find him."

"I know how she feels. With everyone accusing him of doing something she knows he wouldn't do."

"He may not have done anything yet," Hunter said while still facing the window. "He may not do anything at all. He's strong, Fynn. He can resist that thing."

Bailey watched his fist ball up on the bed beside him and bit the inside of her cheek to stop from telling him that if Caleb couldn't resist, then no one could. Maybe Leah would kick him like Amber did and he would snap out of it long enough for her to get away.

"We have to find them soon," Bailey said. "The longer we wait..." She saw his knuckles turn white.

This was killing him inside.

"I think they're here," she said. "In the house."

Hunter turned, eyes wide with surprise and maybe a bit of hope.

"The police searched," he said. "With Mama's blessing. They even checked the attic."

"They wouldn't find anything up there. Beckham's too smart for that. He added space to the house when he realized he'd need it to conceal the bodies and maybe the victims while they were alive." Bailey held out the book she'd found in Fynn's room and showed him the entry. "That's why he wanted the original blueprints. He wanted to see what was different."

"We need those blueprints and not that fuzzy picture from the graveyard."

Bailey drew out her phone and texted Charity, filling her in and asking if she could do her magic. Charity answered immediately.

Already at the library. On it.

"In the meantime, we should search," Hunter said, looking over her shoulder at the phone.

"I want to go up to the attic." Bailey stood.

"You just said the police wouldn't have found anything there." Hunter reached for a pencil on his desk so he could fiddle with it.

"They wouldn't because they were only looking for people. But I think Beckham is preoccupied right now with whatever he's trying to do to Fynn and Leah. That's why he hasn't done anything since we've been back in the house. It's why I was able to find this book."

And why the women were able to help and communicate more easily.

"We have to make Fynn and Leah the priority," Hunter insisted, standing too. "We can't waste time looking at an old chest."

"An old chest that might hold clues. An old chest that he was ready to throw me through a window to prevent me from looking at."

Hunter swallowed, and she watched as he turned her words over in his head, then ran a hand back through his hair again.

"Let's do it."

CHAPTER 20

Together, they marched into the hallway and went straight for the door to the attic. Bailey's heart hammered as they climbed the ladder steps. Once again, a musty rotten scent filled her nose and an invisible weight settled on her stomach and shoulders. She wondered if she'd miscalculated and Beckham really was there, waiting for them, lurking where he knew she'd come.

Bailey glanced at the leaded window at the front of the house, where the sun hit the center as it sunk in the sky. She shivered as the deafening silence felt like a plug in her head.

"It's buried again." Hunter's voice echoed around the space.

Bailey turned her attention to the chest, which again was shoved into an inconspicuous spot, nearly concealed by random boxes, crates, and papers behind the area where the chains still swung slowly, like a bizarre perpetual motion machine.

Without a word, Bailey joined him and they dug out the chest more fervently this time, unable to shake the feeling that Beckham may notice them and attack at any moment. While Hunter pulled the heavy thing, inch by inch, along the floor, Bailey searched the area and settled on a fire extinguisher that probably hadn't been touched since the 50's. She carried it over and Hunter stood back as she brought it down, with all her might, against the metal lock. The clank rang in her ears as she tossed the red canister aside and knelt to find the lock broken. Mouth dry and heartbeat pounding in her skull, Bailey pulled the metal chunks away and reached for one curved side of the trunk while Hunter grasped the other. Together, they pushed.

The first thing that hit her was the smell. It was the rotten scent quadrupled and stale. Bailey pressed her arm to her nose, pulling her face to the side, away from the source. Still, she kept her eyes locked on the horror within. A skeleton, twisted and folded unnaturally to fit inside, partially covered with a pile of clothes stuffed on top of it.

Right away, she recognized the color and pattern of the soft cotton dress Dottie had been wearing in the picture she'd seen. The empty eye sockets stared up at her as though in horror, a rag still tied over the mouth.

"Oh, God," Hunter said. "Oh, God. Is that?"

"Dottie," Bailey whispered. "We found you. Help me get her out of here."

Hunter looked aghast but followed along as Bailey pulled out the wrinkled dress and laid it on the floor like a sheet. Carefully, they reached in and lifted the skeleton as Bailey tried desperately not to think about what her skin was actually coming in contact with. Dottie started to crumble in places, falling apart as they set her on the clothing. Her wrists and ankles were bound behind her, but the bones slipped easily from their joints, and her legs and arms ended up beneath her ribs and pelvis. Bailey's stomach turned and she had to step away for a minute.

"Are you okay?" Hunter didn't sound like he felt much better.

Bailey nodded, not trusting herself to speak, and went back over to the trunk, shining her phone light over the dark recesses. Inside lay a small golden cross on a chain. It had been in the picture as well, at Dottie's throat. Gingerly, Bailey reached for it and laid it next to the corpse on the ground.

"There's more in here." She wouldn't take her eyes from Dottie. "See what else was near the chest."

Behind her came the sounds of heavy things scraping across the floor, punctuated by the occasional grunt.

Then she heard, "I found something."

Bailey turned, and Hunter was standing in the rear of the same area, where the roof slanted so low he was forced almost in half. He pointed at the ground and she squinted in the low light, at the spot where he held his phone out. The floorboards were a different color than the rest, and when she joined him, she saw that there was a joint built into the floor.

"It's a trapdoor," she said, excitedly.

Hunter held the phone in his mouth as he pried it open. Inside were papers and several labeled mason jars filled with what looked like dirt.

"Let's get it all downstairs and call the police about Dottie," Hunter said.

"I hate to leave her here even for a while longer." Bailey glanced back at the skeleton. "But I think you're right. And we need this evidence right now, not the police. They'll never buy the possessed-by-a-ghost defense. You heard Amber. They wouldn't even hear her out."

They gathered as much as they could and carefully made their way down into the second-floor hallway, Hunter going first. Then Bailey handed down the items to him, bit by bit.

"You know these jars are labeled with names, right?" Hunter asked, as she poked her head down to deliver the last one.

Bailey nodded with her eyes closed. She had noticed, and while handling them, she tried not to think about how Paul'd said Beckham had cremated his wives to keep them at the house. But the sooner they got them and Dottie out of the house, the sooner their spirits would be freed. At least, she hoped that was how it worked.

"Watch your step," Hunter said, as she turned to make the descent after him.

But as she reached the first rung, something grabbed hold of her from behind and beneath the arms and yanked her back into the attic.

Bailey screamed as she was dragged backward. *Not again.*

Hunter yelled after her, but she could only watch as the door slammed shut on him and the heaviest boxes slid from all directions to block the top. He pounded against it, making one of the boxes shake, but the blockade held in place.

"Let go!" Bailey screamed, twisting and fighting against her invisible assailant.

Instead of being thrust through the air, toward the window, she was dropped on the ground beside Dottie's remains. After scrambling to her feet, Bailey whirled but found nothing except the sound of her own breath coming heavy and fast.

"Who's here?"

"Don't leave me." The voice swam over her shoulder, pouring ice down her back.

"Dottie?" Bailey whipped around again. "Is that you?"

"Stop him," the voice replied, again from behind, sliding over her skin like the tip of an icicle.

Bailey swung around again. "I'm trying. I found you like you wanted, but you're scaring me."

Three loud thumps sounded from below. Hunter was trying everything to get up there to her.

"Even if I find him, what makes you think I can do anything? He's managed to kill at least a dozen of you. Why am I any different?"

When no answer came, she started texting Hunter, punching at the keyboard so fast she was sure autocorrect was having a field day.

It's Dottie. She doesn't want me to leave. After she typed in the last word, her battery went dead.

The only light source left in the room was gone, as was her only tool of communication, and she was trapped in the attic with at least one ghost, a dead body, and eventually an immortal serial killer.

"Okay." Her voice shook. "It's okay, Bailey. We can handle this."

She let her eyes slowly adjust, watching as shapes appeared out of the darkness, outlining the larger things surrounding her. She gradually turned in place, trying to find something that would give her a clue as to what to do next besides curl into a ball and cry until Hunter found a way to get her out.

Then she saw it. A glowing line of light shining from a thin slat at the base of the wall nearest the rectangle of the large inset window. If there was a light, then there had to be a source. So, Bailey moved toward it, careful not to run into any boxes, or worse, bodies, on the floor. When she got there, she knelt beside the wall, cold air slipping through the old building, from the outside. She passed her hand over the light and found that it was coming from a space behind and possibly below the wall. Was it one of the rooms downstairs that was revealed by the old house settling? Or something else?

Bailey recalled the door she'd asked Fynn about. The one he'd said led to the attic. Maybe this was another way down. Her pulse sped up once again, making her dizzy as she considered the possibility of a second exit. She fumbled in the dark, running her fingers along the crack and up and over the adjacent wall. By feel alone, she found a gap in the wood paneling, bigger than those near it. But how could she get it open? There had to be a latch or a handle if it was meant for a human to get through. So, there had to be something to trigger it. She groped for a knob or handhold where she could gain some leverage as the air around her grew colder and colder, something she'd grown to associate with supernatural energy gathering for some purpose. And, typically, Bailey wasn't thrilled with those purposes, so she worked harder and faster, desperate to find the way out.

The familiar mist gathered on the ground, submerging her legs from the hips down in what felt like a freezer. The mist began to glow, a subtle blue light emanating from everywhere, showing the gaps in the wall, along with all the nooks and crannies around it. Bailey used the light to scan the section of wall for anything that looked like a door handle or trigger. In the movies, there were always books and sliding shelves that revealed hidden passages. But there were no bookshelves here.

Her fingers brushed against some small indentations in the wood. She squinted and ran her hand back over them again, counting. One, two, three, four. Four dents in a semicircle pattern, halfway up the wall. She stood and examined the fingertip-sized clues, sliding the tips of her own inside them.

She turned her head, stretching her thumb to find a fifth indentation below the others. The mist swirled in a circular pattern over the wall, framing her hand in an ever-turning oval. She pressed inward and twisted her hand in the direction of the swirling mist. Somewhere inside the wall, a mechanism popped and the panel swung inward, revealing a narrow winding stairway leading downward toward the glow of yellow light.

The mist dimmed and vanished as Bailey put a tentative foot on the first step. The wood creaked beneath her weight but didn't give way, and she descended slowly into the unknown, hand braced against the cold wall that probably faced the outside of the front of the house. The stairwell was in tight quarters as she wound down, and she found herself in a small hidden room no bigger than a walk-in closet, with a slim, familiar door on the opposite side of her, not ten feet away, that she knew led to the hallway outside the bedrooms. The room was lit by a modern camping lantern set on a small table which also held a collection of dirty old tools and knickknacks, covered in what looked like rust. And on a small cot that resembled more of a hospital bed than bedroom furniture, lay a white sheet outlining the form of a body, unmoving beneath. To the side, on the ground, lay the remnants of what appeared to be Leah's crimson costume, and above the sheet, stretched out and tied to a hook on the wall above the bed, were two pale hands with fake red nails, several of which were broken off.

"Leah," Bailey squeaked, and rushed to pull back the sheet and reveal her face.

The girl's eyes were closed, her mouth slightly open, lipstick smeared across her cheek and over her chin. Dark, angry bruises marred her perfect neck in roughly the same shape as the indentations that opened the room for Bailey.

"Leah." Bailey shook her by the shoulders.

She couldn't be dead. She *couldn't*.

Bailey stopped shaking her and pressed her fingers to Leah's pulse point. An almost nonexistent pulse beat back, each thump representing what she imagined to be a monumental effort to keep going.

Bailey rushed for the door, twisting the knob and pushing with all her might, shoulder against wood. She burst out into the hallway, falling onto the burgundy runner, on her hands and knees, where a commotion stirred to life around her.

"Help her!" she screamed, as Hunter fell to her side and a policeman rushed past her, into the hidden room, and another rushed to her other side, calling for paramedics.

With the relief of Hunter's arms around her and the reassuring knowledge that help was coming for Leah, Bailey finally let the horror and fear of the past hour wash over her, and collapsed against Hunter's shoulder, consciousness giving way.

CHAPTER 21

The strong smell of floral perfume was the first thing to come into focus, followed by the awareness that she lay on something soft, with someone close beside her. Bailey blinked and the world fell into focus, along with the memories she'd wished were nightmares instead.

"Leah," she croaked, trying to sit up, but was met with a wall of vertigo.

"She's alive," her father said, from the chair by her head.

"Dad?" She tried sitting up again, slower this time, and succeeded despite the dizziness and nausea.

"I'm here, Bailey." Her father pulled her hand into his own. "Mrs. Callahan called me."

The scent of cinnamon and strong coffee replaced the roses, and Bailey's stomach settled as Estrella set down a tray on the coffee table between the couch where she was laying and the other seats, occupied by her dad, Hunter, and Sergeant Harper. Estrella poured a mug for Bailey, added sugar cubes and cream, then tucked it into Bailey's hands like a warm hug. Then Bailey sat beside her father and next to Hunter, who leaned toward her like she was magnetic North even though there was a table between them.

"Thank the Lord you're okay," her father said, hysterics barely hidden behind his cracked façade.

"But Leah." Bailey saw those dark marks coloring the girl's throat and could barely hold back the tears.

"She's in the hospital," Sergeant Harper said. "She's in stable condition, but another few hours and she may not have made it. As it is, she won't be telling us the whole story for a while. She's in an induced coma to keep her still while she heals."

"Oh," Bailey said, staring down into her coffee mug, where the tan liquid still swirled from the spoon Estrella had stuck inside.

It reminded her of the mist that helped her find her way to Leah.

"We still haven't located Fynn," Harper continued, leaning forward in his chair, near the other end of the sofa.

"Do you really have to bother her with this?" her father said. "She's barely woken up, and I'm still not convinced she shouldn't be checked out in the hospital."

"I'm sorry, sir. I know how difficult this is for you."

"You have no idea."

"No, sir. You're right. That was a poor choice of words," Harper said and lowered his eyes.

"I don't think Fynn did this," Bailey said.

Estrella let out a whimper, smiling at her with gratitude.

"Did you see him while you were up there?" Harper met her gaze. "Is he the one that grabbed you in the attic and locked out Hunter?"

Bailey glanced over at Hunter, who'd gone into shutdown mode.

"He wasn't there," she said, also trying to let Hunter know she meant Beckham.

"Then what happened exactly?" Harper asked.

"A pile of boxes fell over on the door and I couldn't get back down. So, I had to find another way out. Then my phone ran out of battery. That's when I saw the light from that room, glowing in a crack on the wall. I searched the wall until I figured out what opened the panel and found Leah."

Harper sat back in his chair, chewing on a cookie from the tray. He wasn't buying something. Was Bailey that bad of a liar?

"Maybe he thought he'd killed her, and ran?" Bailey's father seemed relieved to hear that his daughter hadn't been attacked by a madman.

"Fynn didn't do this," Bailey repeated, more forcefully than she meant to. "He couldn't have."

"I know it's hard to believe when someone you know turns out to be a monster," Harper said.

"Innocent until proven guilty?" Bailey's voice was shrill as she stood, shakily.

Harper hung his head, once again abashed. "We have to find him to find the truth. But his fingerprints are all over that room, including the young lady's clothing. And the bruising around her neck matches as well."

Bailey hadn't thought about the physical evidence. And why would Beckham care about that? The more lives he ruined, the better. How could she convince them otherwise? She couldn't let Fynn go to jail for a crime he didn't commit.

"And we're pretty sure other DNA evidence will be a match as well," Harper said. "I'm sorry to have to tell you that."

"He's being framed," she insisted, setting her mug down.

"We'll let the courts decide." Harper stood as well. "Right now, finding him is the most important thing. And I have a couple more questions if you don't mind, Miss Thompson."

Bailey sat back down with a sigh. "What?"

"You found that body in the attic, with Mr. Callahan here?"

Bailey met Hunter's eyes and nodded.

"Why did you move her?" he asked, shaking his head incredulously. "Not only did you tamper with evidence, you could've desecrated a body. Why would you want to touch that?"

"It wasn't right," Bailey said softly. "The way she was stuffed inside that trunk like garbage. I... I just didn't think she should be stuck that way anymore. And her name is Dorothy Radcliffe. I recognized the clothes from a picture I saw when we were researching the house's history, for our paper."

Harper shook his head. "Dorothy was found in that very attic, all right. And those may be her clothes, but that was a different body."

"No, sir." Bailey felt a cold hand on her shoulder and smelled the scent of rose perfume wafting by. "With all due respect, the other body was assumed to be her. Test the DNA or whatever you can do, and you'll find that the other body was a girl named Susan Whitaker, who was reported missing a decade or more apart from Dot—Dorothy's murder."

Everyone in the small gathering sat quietly, aghast.

"Anyway, if I'm not being arrested or something, Hunter and I really need to go."

Bailey stood again and walked around the coffee table to take Hunter's hand.

"Where do you think you're going?" her father said. "It had better not be anywhere near his insane brother. In fact, I think you need to get your butt back home and in bed for the rest of the weekend. I wasn't too happy that you accidentally forgot to mention Hunter's address when we first met."

Bailey squeezed Hunter's hand. "Don't you dare blame Hunter for this. And no, Dad. I'm sorry, but you don't get to suddenly micromanage my time. If it wasn't for us, there'd still be a body in the attic and Leah would be dead. So, I hope you'll trust me enough to let me do what I need to do."

Her father's face went from pale to boiling lobster in about three seconds.

"I believe Sergeant Harper would agree that I do indeed get to micromanage you until you turn eighteen. And although that's soon, it's not yet."

Estrella stood, tsking under breath, and took Bailey's hand, standing between her and her father.

"*Mija*, I appreciate everything you've done for us, but you need to listen to your father. He loves you and he's trying to protect you. I would feel horrible if something happened. Even though I know my son is not the one involved, someone attacked a girl in my own home, and someone is out there hurting young girls. Please, for my sake, go home where it is safe."

Bailey's stubborn indignation got stuck somewhere in her throat as Estrella searched her eyes, looking older and more fragile than she remembered. This had to be so hard for her, coming to this home to make a better, more stable life for her sons, and having one missing, accused of attempted murder, while someone was attacked in her own home.

"Okay," Bailey said.

She'd find a way to help from home. She didn't know where else to look, anyway.

Bailey squeezed Estrella's hand, and though it killed her to go, she let her father lead her home and away from Hunter and the Gallows House.

CHAPTER 22

Bailey sat in her bed, chin on her knees, staring at her phone as it charged. She'd texted Hunter and Charity the moment her dad finally left her alone, but neither had responded yet. Hunter was probably still under the watchful eye of the sergeant, and had Estrella to care for besides. But what about Charity? She needed her best friend more than ever right then.

As if called by unseen forces, the doorbell rang below and she heard the familiar footsteps climbing the stairs. Seconds later, Charity burst into the room, pink glasses pushed up on her small red nose.

"It's cold out there." She shut the door behind her and dropped an armful of papers onto the mattress in front of Bailey before removing her sweater and fingerless gloves.

"You're here," Bailey said.

"Of course. I got your texts, but I figured I'd answer you in person. Much better face to face, right?" She smiled.

Bailey had to agree.

"How's Leah?" Bailey asked.

Charity climbed onto the foot of the bed to face her, cross-legged, with the papers she'd brought in between the girls.

"I was at the hospital as soon as I heard, and believe me everyone else heard, too, judging by the crowd. I couldn't get in to see her, but her parents said she's going to be okay."

"You should've seen her," Bailey said.

She was haunted by the image of her pale face and smeared lipstick. Of the clothes on the floor and the tools that were covered in what she'd thought to be rust, but could've been another dark brown liquid. She was grateful and angry she hadn't seen the rest of Leah beneath the sheet.

"She'd been strangled and…" Bailey said, "and I don't know. It looked pretty bad."

"I'm sorry you had to be the one to find her," Charity said softly. "Fynn's still missing. Rumor is they have Leah's DNA in his truck, and traces of blood."

Bailey winced and looked away. "I can't imagine where he is. I mean, I'm glad he wasn't in that room when I got there, or I don't know what would've happened. Where else could he be? I mean, I found the secret room."

"Maybe not the only one." Charity rifled through the papers on the bed.

She picked out about six and started piecing them together like a puzzle on the mattress.

"I couldn't find the original blueprints, but I found a better picture of Beckham holding them and I blew it up as big as I could, went over the lines with pencil, and blew it up again to get this."

Bailey stood to look at the pictures. It was poor resolution, but there was no doubt this was the blueprint of the Gallows house.

"Holy crap, Charity, this is it."

She hugged her friend and studied the blueprints then dropped to her knees to get closer.

"So, this is the area you found the room, from what I understand." Charity pointed to the area where the chamber was.

It was, in fact, missing from the original.

"Take a look at the grounds," Charity said. "There's something in here I've never seen."

Bailey followed the path Charity traced with her finger. In the middle of the front yard, where the blur was that Paul and his group assumed was a pentagram, was what appeared to be a cellar built apart from the house.

"Where is that?" Bailey asked. "Is that... under the weeping willow?"

"Yep. Like those guys at the cemetery thought. Maybe he really did bury his mom down there and had planned it all along."

The girls both jumped when her father knocked on the door. Bailey dove back in bed, while Charity scooped the papers together before he popped his head in.

"I'm going to run out for some chicken soup for dinner. Is there anything else you girls want?"

"Thanks, Dad, that's great."

Bailey waited for his footsteps to retreat down the stairs. Charity rushed to the bedroom window and watched as Bailey's dad's car drove away. Then she pulled out her phone and texted.

"Hunter's on his way. I'll go let him in." She rushed downstairs.

Bailey shook her head in wonder and waited until the two of them appeared in her doorway.

Hunter hurried to her side, and she flung herself into his arms, pressing her head to his chest.

"Are you okay?" he asked, into her hair. "I thought I'd lost you. I couldn't get back in no matter how hard I tried. I had to call the police. I had no choice."

"It's okay. It's good that you did, because they were there for Leah."

"If you two are done being all romantic and dramatic, I'd like to fill Hunter in on what we found." Charity laid out the pictures again, this time kneeling on the carpet.

She showed him the chamber on the blueprints.

"How do we get inside?" he asked.

"I don't know," Charity said. "I can't figure it out from these. I wish I'd found the originals. It would be a lot easier to read."

"This is amazing," Bailey assured her. "Maybe it has to do with the tree?"

Charity frowned. "When was the tree planted?"

"It had to be there pretty early if he hung himself in it," Hunter said.

"Something's bothering me." Bailey sat back on her bed. "Why would he hang himself? If he's this cold-blooded psychopath who likes torturing women, why would he take his own life, supposedly in grief?"

"Maybe he wasn't the original killer?" Charity said. "Maybe it possessed him, and when it left or whatever, he hung himself?"

"No." Bailey shook her head. "I'm sure it's him. I think he knew he was about to be caught, and rather than take his punishment he... escaped."

Hunter and Charity exchanged a glance. "Escaped?"

"Maybe those witches or whatever were right. Maybe he killed himself there for a reason. Maybe it gave him the ability to stay on and keep killing. I mean, even if it wasn't a pentagram on the blueprint, there was one on his arm."

"So, do you think he's hiding in there?" Charity asked, pointing to the cellar space beneath the tree.

"Fynn?" Hunter asked. "I don't know. It seems like if we get in there, we'll at least find more information."

"Did you bring the ashes?" Bailey asked him.

Hunter got up and retrieved his bag. He pulled out the three labeled jars they'd found in the attic.

"That means five have been released," Bailey said. "Dottie, Susan, and..." she squinted at the labels, "Eugenia, Maureen, and Katherine. We have to scatter their ashes somewhere."

"The cemetery?" Suggested Charity.

"After we find the rest," Bailey said. "There are eight more souls trapped."

"They could be in this space." Hunter pointed toward the blueprints again.

"Only one way to find out," Bailey said. "We better get out of here before my dad gets back."

"When he finds you gone, he's coming after me." He shook his head. "Probably with the entire police department."

"Then I'll tell them I forced you to let me in." Bailey winked.

"We don't have a lot of time," Charity said. "I'll text your dad and tell him I'm taking you with me to have a sleepover and that my mom is giving us dinner."

"Thanks, co-conspirator," Bailey said. "Let's go hunt a ghost."

CHAPTER 23

"There has to be an entrance from the house," Charity reasoned as they speed-walked down Willow.

"But there's also probably one outside somewhere," Hunter said. "There were two ways in and out of the other one, right?"

"Yes," Bailey said. "So, which one do we look for? It could be anywhere in the house, but the one outside could be overgrown by now."

"Not if he's still using it," Hunter said.

"Then let's start with the tree." Charity led the way to the enormous willow, whose branches swayed in the wind, reminiscent of a woman's long hair.

She shone her flashlight toward the roots that buckled out of the ground, and began to walk slowly around the trunk, which was as wide as the three of them put together. Bailey followed close, running her hand along the rough bark, much like she had the wall of the attic when she'd found the finger holds. That couldn't be right. This was a tree, not a manmade home someone could hide a mechanism in like they had the wall inside.

Bailey stopped and stood back from the others, tapping her chin while she thought. What would be something that would stand a chance of lasting centuries and not become overgrown or stumbled upon accidentally?

While passing her own flashlight over the ground, a memory surfaced of the Ouija board and the flying planchette. Maybe it wasn't warning them to get OUT. Maybe whoever it was wanted OUT.

Bailey swung the flashlight beam from the spot on the ground where the board had been to the tree where she remembered the planchette sticking itself. She headed over and nearly tripped on some roots that were shooting above the ground in a large hump. After kneeling down, she passed her hand over the roots. What was forcing them up? Was it natural? She leaned in and felt beneath the mound of root and dirt, scraping the soil, grass, and rocks until she felt something smooth and cold. She nearly jerked away, but realized it was metal she had touched.

"I think I found it," she whisper-called to the others, as she felt for a latch.

Sure enough, further in—a perfect length for someone with the longer arms of a tall man—there was a metal hook, which she looped a finger through and pulled. She jumped back as the ground beneath her began to move. They all watched, flashlights converging on the spot where the ground slid away, followed by what looked like an old piece of thick metal, revealing another narrow set of winding steps. These appeared far more treacherous than the others she'd encountered, as there was no wall to balance against, and no railings either.

"I'll go first." Hunter tested the first step with his weight.

Bailey followed, with Charity behind her, each waiting between going in case the stairs couldn't hold them all at the same time.

"Maybe we should call the police now?" Charity whispered down at Bailey. "Let them know about this place so they can handle it?"

Bailey couldn't do that, though. She knew Charity was scared they'd find Fynn down there, but she also knew the police would never believe it wasn't really him. They had to do this themselves if they wanted to save Hunter's brother.

The stairway went further down than felt natural, and the lower they descended beneath the yard, the more Bailey understood what claustrophobia meant. Feeling trapped in a small space was the least of it, and though she knew this passage or whatever it was had been there since the house was built, she couldn't help but feel that the immense weight of the ground above might collapse on them any moment. Between the darkness, the stale air, and the sense of impending doom, Bailey had to force herself forward with each step, and when they finally reached the bottom, her limbs trembled.

Hunter swept his flashlight over the small earthen room. The ground remained uneven and rocky, as did the walls. There were two metal doors, one leading in the direction of the house, the other in the direction of Lincoln High and Oak street, assuming she hadn't been turned and twisted too much coming down the winding steps.

The sound of their heavy breathing was the only thing that filled the gaping silence, until Hunter gestured toward the door leading to the house, and Charity pointed at the other one.

"Split up," Bailey whispered.

Charity gasped. "That's the thing they always do in horror films and they never make it."

"True." Bailey reached for the door near Charity.

She sucked in a breath and yanked. The door slid open against the dirt, with barely a sound, surprising her, and she peered through while holding out her flashlight. Another dirt passage led about twenty feet forward, then curved to the left. She took a step inside and felt the others fall in behind her. Shallow shelves were dug into the walls on either side, and inside rested several dirty jars, some empty and open, others sealed, all covered in spiderwebs.

"Do you think these are more victims?" Hunter asked.

Bailey didn't have to answer. She just brushed some of the cobwebs away from a sealed jar, and rubbed at the label with her sleeve, revealing a peeling yellowed paper with the name Sheila on it.

"We need to bring these upstairs." She pulled out a satchel she'd brought, that hung empty on her shoulder. "We have to remove them."

"I'll do it." Charity took the bag. "I'll get them out. I'm not sure my heart can take any more of this anyway."

Bailey nodded, liking the idea of rescuing these souls while not giving up the search for Fynn. She handed over the bag and motioned for Hunter to keep following her around the bend.

The rest of the passage was short, slanted, and ended in a second stairwell. Bailey climbed to the top and found what looked like a manhole cover. She pushed, but it was too heavy to lift. Awkwardly, Hunter squeezed in beside her and helped, and together they found themselves peering out at the street level on Willow, near the corner of Oak.

"It's a fake manhole." Hunter slipped back down inside and carefully set it back into place. "Who would question it?"

"An easy way to sneak victims back and forth," Bailey said, stomach tightening as she pictured Susan being dragged this way after being abducted from the school.

And part of the magic of the place was making people want to avoid it. It was probable no one ever bothered to look at this manhole cover, even street pavers who had to work near it.

"Let's go back and check the other door," Bailey said.

Hunter gave her hand a quick squeeze and backed down the steps. By the time they reached the original cavern, Charity was preparing to ascend the steps, with a full bag.

"There were six," she said.

"Wow." Hunter stared at the bulging bag hugged to her chest.

"I'll be careful with them," Charity promised. "There were also several empty jars there, Bailey. Open and... and..."

"What?" Bailey asked impatiently.

"Two of them had labels. One was Amber."

Bailey pressed her eyes shut, unable to speak as she pictured her brother's former girlfriend in place of Leah, with bruises around her throat. A pale, unmoving face.

"What was the other one?" Hunter asked, angrily.

"Bailey," Charity said.

Bailey snapped her eyes open and met Hunter's gaze. The pain and shock in his eyes was clear, but so was the protective determination to save her from some horrible fate.

"I'm fine," she said, more to herself than him.

She'd known Beckham was as obsessed with her as she was with the house, and it wasn't really as big of a surprise as she thought. Its goal was to scare her into submission. But that wasn't going to happen. She was going to stop it from filling any more jars or collecting any more skeletons.

"This is too dangerous." Hunter balled his hand into a fist. "You need to go with Charity."

"What I need to do is go with you to find Fynn. We can save him, Hunter. Caleb didn't have anyone he could trust so he took it upon himself to stop this thing from using his body. Fynn has us. Don't let Beckham win by dismissing me like that."

Hunter contorted his face, and Bailey knew he was worried, but it was Fynn who was in trouble and needed help. She didn't know if she could take it if Hunter sent her away. Because what she'd said wasn't entirely true. Caleb could've chosen to trust her, and he hadn't even seen that as an option.

"Let's go." Hunter motioned with the beam of light, toward the other metal door. "Two is better than one."

Bailey relaxed her shoulders and followed Hunter's lead as Charity climbed the steps behind her. This was it, the door that led to the final two souls, and most likely Travis Randall Beckham himself.

CHAPTER 24

Again, the door slid open like it was used often, and a chill draft swept over them, making their flashlights blink like the batteries inside were mere candle flames flickering in the wind. Bailey held her breath until the beams settled back to the solid-on position, and the two of them crept forward, down a passage similar to the one on the other side, but somehow darker, narrower, and more twisted by the natural obstacles of the earth. Roots and rocks bulged from the sides of the path and they twisted around them, avoiding spiders and an occasional slithery motion in the shadows.

Bailey hadn't considered the mundane dangers of rattlesnakes or black widows when she'd come down there, but she pushed onward in spite of her fluttering heart. This path didn't slope back upward like its counterpart. Instead, it ended at yet another door.

Acknowledging her gut instinct, she wrapped a hand over Hunter's arm and squeezed. He stopped, turned to her, pulled her into his arms and kissed her, lips warm and intense against hers. It made her heart swell and stomach squirm as she melted against him and returned all the pent-up fear and passion he'd put in.

When he pulled away, Bailey realized their faces were wet, but she wasn't sure whose tears they were. Did it even matter?

"I love you, Bailey. I… I wanted you to know how I feel before we go in there. I know it's fast and the timing sucks, but with everything going on, I wanted to be honest with you about my feelings."

Something inside Bailey leaped for joy even though her head screamed that this was the most insane place and time possible to talk about the subject. It was fast and crazy and all of those things, but she'd never felt about anyone the way she felt about Hunter, and she'd never been able to be as open with anyone either, with the exception of Caleb, who it had turned out hadn't been as open with her in return.

"I may just love you, too," she said simply as she reached around him and opened the door.

She froze as her light fell on a glass case on the opposite wall. Inside, two mummified faces stared back at her, black abysses where the eyes should've been, skin glowing yet rotted and puckered like it had been sucked dry. The women had matching brown ratted hair that fell where their shoulders should've been. But they had no shoulders or bodies. They were just heads, suspended in midair, behind the glass.

Hunter stepped up beside her and Bailey buried her face against him, muffling her scream.

"I'm guessing those are his mother and sister," Hunter said.

Bailey pulled her face back out and glanced over the rest of the room, trying to avoid looking in those eye sockets again. Lightheadedness overtook her when she saw the fixture in the corner of the room, placed next to yet another door. It was a chair of some sort, made entirely of what appeared to be polished human bones. And it had a definite pentagram shaped into its back.

"This is beyond sick," Bailey said, trying to keep whatever was in her stomach down.

"We'll tell the police." Hunter pulled her in against him like he could imbue her with strength, even though she could feel him shaking as well.

He moved ahead toward the door, but Bailey stayed where she was. It was like her legs were stuck in cement. She didn't want to go through that last door. She had a bad feeling about it.

"Stop," she said, as Hunter reached for the handle.

He looked back at her, shocked, hand hovering over the door handle.

"Do you need to go back?" Hunter furrowed his bushy brows.

"No." Bailey pressed her eyes closed for a moment to gather her wits about her. "No, I need to finish this. It's probably more of whatever magic makes people avoid the house and even the street."

Hunter held out his other hand for her to join him, and squeezed her reassuringly before swinging open the metal door. Inside was yet another chamber, dark and dense. Distant screams of the past echoed inside Bailey's head as Hunter's flashlight rushed over the walls of what she could only describe as a chamber of horrors. Dark brown stains splattered across the walls, while various ropes and chains hung at different heights, from pullies on the ceiling. In the center was a table much like the one she'd found Leah on, only there were no white sheets, just a yellowed mattress, soaked in the same dark brown as the walls, and now that she looked—the floor. In the center of it was a drain. On the table were old leather straps like she'd seen in movies of asylums from the turn of the century. Spaced to hold wrists and ankles. Rusted trays held frightening-looking tools with pincers and blades.

Bailey let her hand slip from Hunters as he moved into the room, slowly rotating, eyes wide as he explored. He froze facing her, beam pointed above her head, terror on his face. She rushed to his side and turned to see what new discovery could make him look even more disturbed.

All over the wall, ceiling to floor, were names written in the same dark brown that Bailey didn't want to label blood. She recognized almost each one as the victims of Beckham, each at an odd angle in childlike script. She moved her light down the wall, to the corners. She counted sixteen names. All women. Some that matched those she and Charity had found when looking for missing persons in the area. And next to the wall, tucked in the corner, was a strange metal chair, straps open at the handles and feet.

"I think that's an old electric chair," she said, as Hunter continued sweeping the room with his flashlight.

"There's another door," He said in a raspy voice.

Bailey walked to the spot he indicated and opened it. Inside was another winding stairway, and she started to climb.

Something was bothering her. They'd found his hideout and he no longer had Leah, so why wasn't he coming after them?

"It's a really tall one," Bailey called back, feeling as though she'd climbed several stories by the time she reached a trap door above her head.

She was so twisted and turned, she had no idea where she was. She waited for Hunter to catch up, and together they shoved it open. It was difficult, like something was pushing against them from the other side. She took the flashlight from Hunter and he shoved with all his might, finally letting them see it was underneath a heavy carpet. He held it up as high as he could while Bailey climbed through and worked her way out from under the rug, with the intent of rolling it back so Hunter could get through more easily. When she made it through to fresh air, she was shocked to find herself in the middle of Hunter's room upstairs.

"Bailey?" Hunter called.

She snapped out of her shock enough to pull the heavy rug back and let him out.

"You never knew what was right below your room?"

She watched his face register surprise, then close off.

"I hate this house." He stuffed his hands in his pockets and plopped on the bed.

Before Bailey could respond, her pocket buzzed like crazy. Hunter's must've done the same, because he dug out his phone as well. A million texts rolled across the screen as they came in now that they'd found a pocket of reception. Bailey's blood ran cold as she read the first from Charity.

Did you get the message from Estrella? I had no reception down there. Fynn turned himself in to the police. Come quickly. I'll wait by the tree.

Bailey flinched as Hunter flung his phone down on the bed in fury.

"What the hell?" he said. "They're going to put him away for something he didn't even do. I have to go."

"Wait a minute What do you mean you have to go? *We* have to go."

"Look, Bailey, I appreciate everything. But this is a family thing."

"Yeah, and I want to help."

Hunter closed his eyes and stuffed his hands and cell deep in his jean pockets. When he spoke, his voice had a low tremor in it she'd never heard.

"I know you mean well, but you don't know what it's like. You can't know what it is to have your guilt decided by people before you even get a word out, just because of who you are. You heard that officer. He already has Fynn put away for attempted murder."

Bailey's throat dried up, making it impossible to respond with more than, "But…"

She may not have been in that situation, but she sure as hell understood what it was like to have a family member accused of something you were sure he didn't do.

Hunter put up a palm and shook his head, refusing to meet her eyes.

"I have to go. I don't have time for this right now."

Not an hour earlier, he'd said he loved her. They'd been through hell and back together, and now he was ready to ditch her like she was nothing? She cared about his family, too, not just him. She wanted to be there for Estrella and Tom, and especially Fynn, who was in the same situation Caleb had been in. Caleb, who'd felt trapped and frightened and saw no way out other than to take his own life.

Hunter shoved a ballcap on and headed toward the hall, completely in his own world. She reached out a hand as he walked out. She wanted to tell him he wasn't alone and that she really did understand. That he didn't have to do this without her. But something wouldn't let her.

Caleb hadn't let her in, hadn't trusted her with the secrets that had consumed him. If he had, things may've been different. Caleb hadn't believed she could help, either. He'd only thought of her as another dangerous thing to worry about. A burden. And maybe he was right. Maybe, despite all her good intentions, she was just another victim being manipulated by the Gallows House. No one else had ever overcome the evil there. Why should she be any different?

A tear leaked from her eye and splattered on the top of the trapdoor exposed beneath the rolled-up carpet. Bailey hugged herself, shivering in the cold she hadn't even realized had crept up on her during her reverie. Through the almost imperceptible edges of the trapdoor, white mist seeped into the room, gathered over her feet, and twisted up and around her body in something like a cold hug.

"I don't want to become one of you," Bailey whispered. "I'm sorry. I don't know what else I can do. I found all your remains and will make sure the police take the rest of them out of here. But there's nothing I can do to stop Beckham for good."

The lamp on Hunter's desk began flickering, and a strong wind howled through the room. Bailey stood firm, not appreciating the temper tantrum when she'd done so much for them already. She waited as the wind swept her hair across her face and the lightbulb exploded, shattering a storm of glass over the surface of the desk.

"I really wish you could use all that energy to just talk to me." Frustration filled her eyes with more tears.

"They can't," a voice whispered over her ear.

Bailey spun around to find a girl about her height, with almond colored tendrils of hair parted in the center of her head and spilling loose over her shoulders and back. She was dressed in a flowing ankle-length cotton dress covered in flowers. Her eyes glowed blue and her skin was slightly translucent despite the clear pattern on her shift. The scent of rose perfume filled the air.

"Dottie?" Bailey recognized the face staring back at her. "You're here. I mean, you can talk to me?"

Dottie smiled and laughed. "It does take some energy and concentration to be here, so I can't stay long. But yes, now that you freed me. Thank you, Bailey."

"Tell me everything," Bailey burst out. "What happened? Why can't the others talk? Why can you?"

"You freed me. You found my body and released me from the house. He yearns for control. He demands it in life. He dominates our bodies, our minds, even our souls. He found a way to capture us beyond death. To hold us here and use our energy to make himself stronger."

"So, he keeps his victims here by keeping their bodies, and he has so much control over them that they can't, well, do what you're doing?"

Dottie started to fade, her dress becoming as transparent as the rest of her so that Bailey could see the wall through her.

"We are like batteries to him. He takes what he needs, and when we fight, when he sees we've interfered, he punishes us. That's why we can't help directly. I took quite the punishment when I helped you on the stairs. Don't worry. It was worth it."

Bailey recalled seeing her face in the mirror, and the dark spot on her cheek that looked like a bruise.

"Only those of us that have been released can act freely. We can't do much on our own. He's very powerful, but you have weakened him, Bailey, by taking away much of his power."

"How do we get rid of him?" Bailey asked, desperate as Dottie practically disappeared in front of her.

"Free us all," Dottie said as she faded from view.

Bailey panicked, reaching for her, but her voice still lingered.

"Only his mother and sister remain. You're almost all free," Bailey yelled.

"He's wounded and like an animal. He's dangerous. He'll lash out," Dottie warned, her voice dissipating into the air.

"Thank you, Dottie." Bailey called, hoping the other girl could hear her, though she felt her presence leave.

She finally had straight information. Something tangible she could do. The only problem was she thought she'd already done it.

CHAPTER 25

Whatever Hunter's wishes were, Bailey had business at the police station, so when she wasn't able to find Charity where she said she'd be, Bailey went on her own to find Sergeant Harper. Now, she couldn't help but see Estrella's strained face and bloodshot eyes from her seat in the corner, with her two youngest sons on either side of her, holding her hands and huddled together like they didn't belong. And they didn't. They'd already been through this pain once with Hunter's father. Maybe Charity had tried to tag along with Hunter, too, only to have him chase her away as well. She sent off a quick text to her friend.

"Miss Thompson." Sergeant Harper sat at his desk, the largest of the few scattered around the room. "How can I help you?"

"Hi, Sergeant. Thanks for seeing me. I'm afraid I found some more evidence at the house."

Sergeant Harper's white eyebrows lifted and he pushed his glasses up on the bridge of his nose.

"And by *the house*, I assume you mean…"

"The Gallows House," Bailey finished for him. "Actually, it's below the house. There's a secret passage under the willow tree that leads back to the house, and there are bodies in it."

"I see." Harper sat back in his chair and swiveled to glance at the Callahan family, then back again with a big sigh. "Normally—if we can even use that word here—when someone finds a body, they call emergency. I don't think I've ever had someone come in here as calm as you are and report it like you'd found a missing watch on the side of the road."

Bailey shifted awkwardly.

"Considering this isn't the first secret room or horrible thing you happen to have found at the house, I'll assume you're getting used to it, which I find incredibly sad and upsetting, Miss Thompson."

Bailey looked down at her hands in her lap, feeling excessively awkward.

"You need to remove the bodies as soon as you can," she said.

"That, I agree with," Harper said. "As soon as we get the scene tagged and investigated. Now, I think maybe you and I should have a bit more of a discussion about the house. You don't mind, do you?"

"You won't like what I have to say," Bailey whispered, raising her head enough to see the Callahan family again, like she had a secret window to look in on their private pain.

It felt wrong, like she was a voyeur, so she met Sergeant Harper's gaze instead.

"It's not my job to hear pleasant things, unfortunately."

Bailey nodded.

"Good. Now where to start?" Harper asked.

"How about with Fynn? He's innocent."

Harper drew his lips into a thin line, like he was trying hard not to yell.

"See? I told you that you wouldn't like it," Bailey said while examining the contents of Harper's desk.

A calendar still stuck on October, with scribbles and yellow rings of coffee stains all over it. A stapler, pen holder, piles of papers, and a picture frame with his kids and grandkids in it. A tiny set of boy-girl twins stared back at her, with dimpled faces and shiny blue eyes.

"I'd very much like it if that were true, Miss Thompson," Harper said, leaning forward on his desk so he'd be in her field of vision again. "What can you tell me that will contradict a full confession and physical evidence?"

Bailey swallowed. "What if I told you all the stories about the house were true, and that not only is it haunted, but I know who the killer is and how he's done it all along?"

Harper stared back at Bailey, tapping a pen against his desk as she stared back, determined and unblinking, willing him to believe her.

"I'd say I need a fresh cup of coffee."

He stood, took a stained mug that read *Best Grandpa* from a printer stand to his left, then retrieved the dregs of the community coffee pot from the corner opposite the Callahans. After dumping a fair amount of sugar inside, he returned to the desk, sat down, leaned back, took a sip, and gestured for her to continue.

She told him everything, knowing she sounded insane, and hoping that living in Shadow Springs himself, there was some shred of possibility that Harper would believe her.

When she finished, Harper drained his mug and set it down, adding a new coffee stain to his collection. He nodded slowly, glanced back at where the Callahans had been seated, now missing, presumably visiting Fynn, then back at Bailey.

"Do you believe me?" She was unable to contain her nerves.

"Yes."

Relief washed over Bailey's entire body so fast that she started trembling.

But before the tears started, he added, "Unfortunately, I can't use any of that in court."

"Wait. So, you believe what I'm telling you, that it's been Beckham all along, and you're still going to put Fynn in jail?"

Disbelief made Bailey's voice rise, and for the first time a few people looked over at her.

"What I'm saying, Miss Thompson, is that I need irrefutable evidence that Mr. Callahan is lying about his confession and that it was someone else."

"So how do we prove it was a ghost possessing him?" Bailey leaned forward so no one else could hear.

"*We* don't." Harper grimaced. "You let the police do our job and believe that justice will be served."

"You're sending me away?" Bailey jolted up to her feet.

First Hunter, now Harper?

"This is no place for a teenage girl. You've seen enough already. And by your own admission, you're in personal danger. Trust the professionals for once and go home to your father. You should know that he called earlier, worried sick."

Bailey froze, stunned. Everything he'd said was true, but she couldn't turn her back on everything now. And the minute she went home, she'd be grounded permanently.

"Can I talk to Fynn?" she asked.

"No." Harper focused on some paperwork on his desk.

Bailey's mouth hung open. She stayed for another minute, during which Harper never looked up, and she knew there was no more for her there. But she wasn't ready to leave yet. She wanted to find the

Callahan's. She knew Hunter had told her to stay away, but she wanted to tell Estrella that she knew Fynn was innocent.

Taking advantage of everyone's endlessly busy monotony, Bailey followed the signs leading to the booking and holding area. Shadow Springs was a small town compared to most of California, so the station matched accordingly. It wasn't hard to follow the sound of hushed voices and occasional sobs from Estrella. She passed by the empty guard desk and into the holding area, where she saw them gathered at a small wooden table. Hunter, Estrella, and Tom on one side, Fynn in an orange jumpsuit, hands cuffed, on the other. His usually impeccable appearance was mussed, his face pale and drawn. Even his slouched body language spoke of someone who'd given up hope.

Bailey rushed toward them and they all looked up. A few steps forward and she was grabbed by the arm so hard it yanked her backward. Her first thought was that Beckham had come to the station to get her, but when the guard spun her around to face him, she realized the source was far from paranormal.

"You are not allowed back here," the man said.

"She's with us," Estrella said, standing.

"Family only," the guard answered, still holding Bailey's arm with a painfully firm grasp.

"She is part of the family. She's my niece," Estrella lied smoothly.

The guard appeared dubious, but finally released her to join the others. Tom smiled at her, and Estrella pulled her into a hug as Hunter stood silently behind them, hands in pockets, stoic and still. It was so hard to read him. Was he angry she came? Glad?

"I don't want to intrude," Bailey said, softly. "But I had to come. Fynn is innocent, and I know it."

Estrella hugged her tighter, then released her only to take her face in her hands, eyes glowing with pride.

"You are not intruding. You are part of our family, Bailey. Thank you for standing with us."

Bailey's shoulders released the strain she'd been holding, and she smiled back, finally feeling needed and appreciated.

"Bailey," Fynn said, in a weak voice that made her turn to him, still holding Estrella's hand. "I don't remember any of it. I was drunk. I did horrible things."

"No," Bailey said, anger flaring inside her. "He wanted you to think that, but you didn't. Hunter, didn't you tell him what happened?" She faced the boy who'd professed his love mere hours ago.

Everyone else turned to face Hunter as well.

"He won't even listen," Hunter said.

Only the skin tightening at his temples gave away the strain he felt inside.

"I need to take responsibility for my actions," Fynn said. "I'm not trying to make up stories or excuses. Not like Dad did. I'll take my medicine like a big boy. It's what I deserve."

Estrella reached toward her eldest son. "*Mijo—*"

"No, Mama. I'm just sorry I hurt you. I never meant to."

Hunter grabbed Bailey's hand and pulled her outside after him.

"I can't look at him anymore. I can't believe he's giving up like that."

"Hunter." Bailey wanted to hold him and comfort him.

"Let's go home." He wouldn't look directly at her. "Will you stay with me a while?"

"Of course." She took his hand again and began the walk toward the exit. "Did you see Charity? She's not answering my texts."

Hunter shrugged. "No. She probably went home, to bed. I'm sure she'll text tomorrow."

"I guess, but it's weird," Bailey said, taking out her phone to double-check. "She'd said to hurry and meet her by the tree."

"So? She flaked. Like everyone does." Hunter spit the words.

Bailey glanced at him, catching his profile, and again saw the strain on his face. He always held it all inside, but maybe this was too much. Maybe he felt like she did, like everyone was always abandoning him when he could've been there to help. Fynn was doing to him what Caleb had done to her. Protecting him instead of letting him in. While that was no reason to take it out on Charity, she didn't think this was the right time to talk about that.

"I'll text her in the morning," Bailey agreed instead, sticking her phone back in her pocket.

There was nothing Charity could do to help at this time of night, anyway.

With Hunter, Bailey entered the house and climbed the steps. She followed him into his room where the rug lay pulled back on the ground, unable to hide its secrets anymore.

"Did you text anyone about what we found?" Hunter sat on his bed and took off his sweatshirt.

"No." Bailey kicked off her shoes and plopped down on the bed next to him.

She wasn't sure if she should tell him about her conversation with Harper. Would it upset him?

"How about your Dad?" he asked, standing to stretch and pull off his T-shirt, revealing the smooth muscles of his back and arms.

"The second I see him he's going to tear me a new one. So, I'm laying low for now."

Bailey remembered the defined abs cut into the front view of Hunter, and quickly chided herself. This wasn't the time to make-out. His brother was in serious danger.

She climbed onto her knees and put her hands on his shoulders, kneading into the knots she knew were there. Hunter let out a sigh, rolling his head back, letting his mass of curls tickle the tops of her hands as she worked.

"So, what are we going to do about Fynn?" Bailey asked after a minute of silence.

"*We* aren't going to do anything." Hunter turned and pulled her in for a kiss.

For a moment, Bailey was stunned. Then she realized what he meant as she answered his hungry mouth with her own. It was that word again. *We*. Hunter didn't want her involved anymore, and that hurt. He obviously wanted something from her, though, because he was putting all his concentration into what he was doing.

He pressed his mouth hard against hers, tongue thrusting into her mouth as he laid her back on the bed, landing one knee between her legs and a hand down over her breast. He'd never moved so fast and rough before, and Bailey had to work her head away and to the side to catch her breath. He didn't seem to mind though, since his mouth continued on to her exposed neck, sucking and nipping at the skin.

"Ouch," she said when his teeth caught her too hard. "Slow down there, buddy. I know you don't want me involved, but I really think we should talk about Fynn."

"I told you," Hunter said, letting his hot, fast breath wash over her ear. "We're letting him take the fall."

"What?" Bailey went cold and realized something was very, very wrong.

She turned her head to look at him as he took her hands in his and jerked them above her head, pressing them down with all his strength so she couldn't move. It wasn't Hunter staring down at her with that gloating, lascivious grin and swirling black eyes.

Bailey's vision blurred as her heart threatened to push through her ribcage.

"Don't pass out," he said, in Hunter's voice. "It's no fun when you aren't conscious, and I have so much to pay you back for, Bailey."

CHAPTER 26

Bailey fought to stay focused—not because it was what he wanted, but because if she passed out, she'd miss any minor opportunities to free herself from the situation. She had to stay smart and alert, remain calm despite her body trembling with fear as she pictured the bruises on Leah's neck, and the heads of his sister and mother bobbing behind glass below them.

"How?" she managed to breathe.

"How did I get inside loverboy?" he asked for her, lowering his face until all she could see were his eyes. "Like I do all the weak ones, including your brother. I wait until they're emotionally unstable, and then they're ripe for the taking. They don't deserve their bodies. They don't use them to their advantage."

"My brother wasn't weak." She found some fire still within her. "He got rid of you long enough to take away your opportunity to use him to hurt people."

Beckham took both her wrists into one of Hunter's large hands, and used the other to squeeze her face, holding it still so she couldn't move her head. His fingers dug painfully into her jaw.

"Weak. He gave up his life, his future, because he was afraid to embrace real power."

Bailey held her words, afraid of what he might do if she made him any more off-balance.

"Good girl, Bailey. Hold your tongue if you don't want it cut out of your body. Yet."

Her trembling intensified, and he grinned wider.

"I'm going to tell you what I tell them all," he said, cocking his head to examine her face. "If you behave and do as you're told, you will suffer less and live longer. Suffer *less*, Bailey, not, not at all. See, you're a special case. You've already caused far too much trouble for me. You've destroyed so much of what's taken me more than a century to build. So, for that, you will be punished either way.

And make no mistake, you will be mine for eternity, just as my dear mother will always be." He leaned down over her face, and whispered in her ear, "I am going to enjoy this. I've been waiting quite a while for you."

Then he laughed. The horrible guttural sound that bounced around the room and off the walls. The same sound she remembered when he'd pushed her down the stairs. He let go of her face and slapped her across the cheek as he continued to laugh like the madman he was.

Think. She remembered Amber's story about kicking Caleb and snapping him out of it. But as she struggled and kicked, she realized he had her completely pinned down. He knew what he was doing. He'd had too much practice, and it had taken Amber God knew how long to find that opportunity. Bailey didn't want to find out what could happen between now and then—if that moment ever even presented itself.

"Let's go somewhere more comfortable." He threw her to the ground.

The wind got knocked from her body, and Bailey screamed at herself to get up and fight. That's when a kick to her abdomen sent her into a fetal position, where she struggled for breath as he threw open the trap door, then grabbed her by the hair to lift her and sling her over his shoulder.

Bailey screamed, finally finding her voice as she scratched and pounded on Hunter's back. But he seemed impervious to her struggle, even enjoying it as he whistled while he carried her down into his torture chamber, and tossed her down the last handful of steps, onto the cold dirt floor.

Coughing, Bailey pushed against the uneven ground, trying to get into a standing position as Beckham ignored her, lighting a lantern sitting to the side so the room flooded with enough light to see its horrifying contents. He began testing various chains and ropes that swung from the ceiling. She crawled away from him and scrambled to a standing position, searching for a weapon, but he was already by the tray of instruments, smiling at her.

"Looking for these? I'll tell you what. I'll let you pick one, and if you can get away, great. If not, that'll be the first thing we play with."

Bailey backed up against the wall, sure it was a bad idea to go for anything on that tray. What would she do if she got hold of one? Hurt Hunter? She couldn't do that. This wasn't his fault and he wasn't going to die like Caleb or end up in jail like Fynn.

He *wasn't*.

Bailey calculated the layout of the room. She again forced herself to stay as calm as possible, and stood up straight, meeting his gaze.

"Promise?" She pretended to play his sick game.

"Oh, yes," he said, stepping back further and spreading his hand out as if showing off a prize on a game show.

Bailey took a deep breath, grabbed the doorknob behind her, and ran as fast as she could, yanking the bone chair onto its side behind her to try and slow him down. She rushed past the heads glowing in the glass and made it through the next door into the dark. No way she'd make it all the way up and out of this maze before he reached her. She'd have to hide, hope he passed her by, and double back. It was her only hope. But the next passage was just that, a short insane hall of sorts, so she dashed right into the door as she scrambled for the handle.

She was sure it had been easy to open when they'd come through, yet as she grappled with it, trying to pull it open, it remained shut. She yanked with all her might as the door on the other end of the passage burst open and light from the lantern swung around the dirt hall, reflecting off the metal of the door she struggled with.

"Don't you think others have tried?" He moved closer, taking his time as she pulled with all her strength and made it open about a foot.

"Do you think it's an accident that the door sticks like that from this direction? That only a man is strong enough to open it?" He laughed, softly this time.

Bailey stopped yanking, stood straight, and hooked her hands around the edge of the door.

"Maybe that's how it was last century," she said, "but a lot has changed since you were alive."

Bailey pulled, putting her feet up against the dirt wall for leverage, and the door opened just enough for her smaller form to slip through. She dashed around it as he reached for her, grabbing hold of the material of her shirt. The buttons down the front popped like tiny bullets and she let it slip off her shoulders as she continued to run, leaving it behind. She got to the stairs she'd last seen Charity on, and tripped over something at the bottom, landing hard on the dirt. The door shoved open and Hunter's body stood there, the lantern swinging again, and the light passed over the area enough for her to see what she'd fallen over. It was the bag she'd brought earlier, open with jars of ashes, some still inside, some rolled out over the ground like they'd been dropped or thrown.

Panic rose again and Bailey's chest hurt with each breath she drew. She stared at the bag and its contents, trying to process what it meant, knowing she should be up and running, but she couldn't move.

"Where's Charity?" she asked.

Beckham reached her and stood above, holding the swinging lantern. The moving lights made the sickness growing in her stomach even worse, and she stood awkwardly to face him.

He cocked his head again, eyes glowing in the dim light. "Would you like to see her?"

"What did you do to her?" Bailey screamed.

He grabbed her wrist and strode away, dragging her behind him, back toward where they'd come from.

"Imagine when I changed bodies, to find a text from that little bitch friend of yours, saying to meet her at my tree. I left you in the bedroom to come back to my lair, only to find Charity by the open door, attempting to remove what I worked so hard to procure. And when you'd already taken so many hard-earned souls from me."

They reached the door to the torture chamber and he swung it open, tossed Bailey through to the inside and onto the floor once again.

"Obviously, she had to make up for one of the souls you managed to release."

"You killed her?" Bailey asked, the world spinning around her.

"Not yet. I like to do things slowly, if you haven't noticed. It's so much more fun. If you don't want to watch me toy with her, then come over here for me like a good girl."

He motioned for her to sit up on the awful table. She hesitated but had to see that Charity was all right. Forcing her shaking legs forward, she got to the table and pulled herself up on it in a sitting position. He smiled and reached above her to pull down some rope that made a terrible squealing sound from whatever pully it was attached to. Bailey winced.

"Raise your hands," he said, leaning over her.

She started to comply, but could only raise them in front of her, too frightened and confused to finish. She wouldn't be able to help Charity if she were no better off. He grabbed her hand and yanked it upward to tie a prepared noose around her wrist. Bailey's elementary school martial arts training kicked in and she shoved with her other hand while kicking with her feet. Unlike the real Hunter, Beckham seemed to be anticipating this and pressed his body against her knees so they didn't go anywhere, and to her frustration, ignored her punches and attempts to scratch at him. She cursed herself for not continuing on past yellow belt.

He whistled again as he got hold of her other hand and finished binding her wrists, then stepped away and yanked on something, causing her to rise into the air, held in place by her hands. She screamed and wheeled her feet, feeling as though her shoulders were being pulled from their sockets. He wrapped his arms around her waist from behind and guided her to the center of the room, where she dangled several feet off the floor, sobbing.

"Starting to accept your position?" He tsked. "Good. Well, as promised, here is your friend. Don't worry, you two will be together for eternity."

He strode over to the corner near the door and pulled an old tarp away, revealing the ancient electric chair they'd found when they first discovered the room. In it was Charity, unconscious, with silver duct tape over her mouth, her hands and feet strapped to the chair. Her clothing was torn and dirty, with scratches in the open areas like she'd been dragged over something sharp. Her pink glasses lay on the ground at her feet at an odd angle, as though they'd been purposely smashed.

"No time for a nap." He repeatedly slapped Charity across the face until she began to revive.

When she spotted him, her eyes grew large, panic drawing all over her face as she struggled against her bonds.

"Charity," Bailey called.

But her friends' eyes grew bigger when she spotted Bailey dangling in only her bra and jeans. Strangled sounds fought to escape from her throat as she struggled harder. Beckham grabbed a handful of Charity's hair and yanked her head back so she was looking at him instead of Bailey.

"This is what happens to girls who get involved in things that aren't their business."

Before Bailey could register what was happening, he had his hands around Charity's throat and his knee in her stomach as he squeezed, making her whole body shake as she struggled to breathe.

"Stop!" Bailey screamed. "Stop. I'll do whatever you want. Please."

He stopped squeezing, but kept his hands in place at Charity's throat. "See?" He looked up at Bailey. "I told you I could make you say please."

Bailey froze in horror. She knew, but she didn't really understand until right that moment that it wasn't Fynn she'd spoken to in the back of the police car.

"Please, please, please," she repeated calmly. "Let go."

He released Charity's neck and stepped away with his hands in the air as Charity sucked in air through her nose and between garbled sobs.

"You are a smart one, aren't you, Bailey?" He strode toward her.

"What is it you want?" she asked, as he put his hands on her hips. "I mean, besides collecting souls for power. Why is it always women? Why not keep the men that don't work out?"

"Because women were made for men's service and pleasure," he said and undid the button on her jeans. "It was something my mother taught me when she was making excuses for the men she brought over and the money they gave her. It was the reason she let them touch me and my sister as well."

Sick swelled in Bailey's stomach as he spoke. She stayed still as he pulled off her jeans and tossed them onto Charity's lap.

"The problem was, I wasn't a woman. I was a man like them, and I deserved to be the one *doing*, not to be the one to have that done to. Are you done psychoanalyzing my horrible childhood yet, Bailey? Do you feel sorry for me now?"

"You're a monster," she said, trying to kick him, but succeeding only in making herself start to swing and spin on the ropes.

He laughed, stepped back, and watched as she swung to face him again.

"Any other questions? As long as you're polite, I'll answer." He selected something from the tray as she again spun away.

"By polite, you mean subservient."

"Perhaps." He stopped her by grabbing her waist as she faced away from him.

"You killed your mother for obvious reasons."

He tied her ankles together.

"What about your sister?"

"She went right to work pleasuring men, the same as Mother, but she refused to take me as a client."

Bailey couldn't speak as bile rose in her throat and his hands rose along her bare legs to her hips once again, before turning her to face him.

"You think the same way she did." He stopped her from swinging and backed toward the tray.

The way normal humans think. "Why the others?"

"The first few were only prostitutes and they were accidents. I like it rough. I suppose I've always enjoyed watching others struggle." He began holding up various instruments and examining them in front of her, whether in sincerity or intimidation, she didn't know. She just kept talking, convinced that if he kept the conversation going, she'd be okay.

"Then your wife?"

He glanced at her, a scalpel held high. "I didn't want to kill Eugenia. She was a good subservient woman, as you suggested. Raised to please and care for her husband. Then she began to complain, as most of you do."

"Complain?" Bailey echoed and stared at the light glinting off the blade in his hand.

"It's like you keep me prisoner in this house," he mocked. "All you want is a slave, not a wife."

"So, you killed her?"

He moved toward her with the scalpel in hand. "No. I'm not unreasonable. I simply kept her in her chambers so she'd see what it really meant not to have any freedom. She kept her life until I caught her with a male servant in our bed, upon my arrival home." He raised the blade to her stomach.

"What's with all the pentagrams?" Bailey burst out, after spotting one on the wall over his shoulder, written in blood, with the names of the victims.

He stopped, blade centimeters from her skin. She held her breath until he pulled it back, letting it rest at his side as he stepped back to look in her face. It hurt so much to see Hunter there. She wanted with every fiber of her being to drive Beckham from his body.

"What do you know about that, little girl?" he asked, voice even and menacing.

Bailey hesitated, searching for the correct answer or whichever one would make him forget the scalpel in his hand.

"The souls I released are angry with you," she said, carefully. "They may not be strong enough to hurt you, but they can give the living information."

He narrowed his eyes as he considered her words. "You've caused a lot of problems, Bailey. I have to admit that I wouldn't have thought a girl like you could uncover so much of my eternal arrangement."

"You're pretty weak, now that I think about it."

"Oh?"

"You need someone else's body to do your dirty work. You aren't strong enough without it."

Wind whirled through the small chamber, kicking up stones and dirt and whipping up Hunter's hair around his head like a personal tornado as he stepped forward, eyes glowing red.

"You think that, do you?"

"That's right." Bailey's stomach was tight, and she wasn't at all sure about what she was saying.

"I use these bodies to make it worse for my victims, not because I'm in need of them. Don't you recall how I almost killed you in the attic? On the stairs?"

Bailey *did* recall.

"I'm still alive, though. You weren't strong enough to finish me off and do all the terrible things you seem to want to do without a body. Face it, you aren't strong enough on your own."

The wind intensified, sending debris to pummel the skin of her mostly bare body. Then he smiled, a wicked smile that didn't belong on Hunter's face, almost as though his lips stretched farther than they should be able to.

"Nice try, Bailey. But no. You see, when their beloved attacks them, they can't believe it. They don't fight as hard at first. They think love will win, until they learn that their lover is like any other man." He reached her again. "Why? is what they always ask as they draw their last breath. That is, if they're still able to speak."

"I already know you aren't Hunter."

Bailey's heart thundered as he took hold of her neck from behind.

"It's also convenient for the living to believe one of them was responsible," he said. "And if you must know, it feels good to be inside a body again. I only gave mine up when I realized the authorities had figured it out and were coming for me. I had to die here on the grounds, or I couldn't have managed all this."

Exactly as she'd thought.

"You're pure evil," Bailey said, as he lifted the blade between them.

"I am simply trying to take what is rightfully mine, and teach some spoiled tramps a lesson in the meantime. Face it, Bailey, you know it's not Hunter doing this, but part of you will never forget that it was his body that hurt yours. You'll always remember this moment."

He flicked the scalpel, slicing the skin above her breastbone. It wasn't deep, but the cut was clean and sudden and very, very real. Blood spurted out, spattering the back of his hand and rolling down her chest as Charity's muffled cries rang out from behind Hunter.

Bailey pictured all the women he'd killed in the body of someone they knew and trusted. How they would have pled and accused without knowing—until it was too late.

That meant she had something none of them had. She could still love and trust Hunter. She *knew* it wasn't him.

"You want me to hate Hunter, but I don't. I won't. I love him."

"Indeed?" He held the edge of the blade up near her cheek, keeping it steady.

Bailey gulped air. "It doesn't matter what you do to me. It won't change my feelings."

"It's just an added bonus. I don't really care about your feelings." He pressed the flat side of the scalpel against her skin, its cool pressure making her breath come faster.

"You don't, but Hunter does," she said, staring into the red eyes, trying to find some part of the man she knew inside.

The quiet, sweet, passionate, real Hunter.

He paused. "Too bad he can't hear you." He pulled her against Hunter's body as he slid the metal down past the stinging and still bleeding cut, to rest at her bra line.

"Keeping him safe from guilt, huh?" She tried to force her voice steady.

He smiled down at her and released her, finally pulling the scalpel back. "Very clever, Bailey. You wouldn't be trying to trick me into letting him out, would you?"

Bailey's heart sank. It was exactly what she was trying to do. She had to reach him. She caught Charity's eye over Hunter's shoulder, the glassy look of terror that met her stole what was left of her confidence.

"Feeling despondent?" Beckham pinched her wounded skin between his fingers, bringing tears to her eyes and her attention back to him. "What you need to understand is that you were never going to win this game. I will always be stronger and smarter."

Bailey forced herself to look at Charity again. This time, it was determination that she saw on her friend's tear-stained face. She read the silent message. *Don't give up.*

"You know that if you let Hunter see this, he'll be strong enough to break free." She was unable to stop the fear in her voice from betraying her.

"Very well, Bailey. Maybe I'll let him watch what I do to his *love*." He reached the blade toward her bra again. "Don't get your hopes up, though. I've done it with others. We'll start by taking off the rest of that material so we have a clean canvas to work with."

"Hunter!" Bailey said, desperation in her voice. "Hunter, I know you're in there."

He laughed again, but Bailey saw his hand tremble slightly, the blade hanging in the air millimeters from her skin.

"You can hear me. I know you can. I love you, Hunter, and I know you love me."

"Love," he spat, slicing through the material of her bra. "Don't you think they've tried that before? *But you love me*," he mimicked, breaking through the strap that seemed to fall away like it was made from no more than butter.

"The others… they thought it was their loved one doing this," Bailey said, keeping eye contact. "They didn't know he was just as much a victim. I know Hunter is hurting the same as I am right now."

His mouth snapped shut, and she knew she had something.

"Hunter, it's okay. I know you aren't in control. But I also know you're in there. You are strong. The strongest, sweetest guy I know. You can stop this. You can save me and your brother."

"Shut up!" he screamed, then smacked her across the face so hard stars burst across her vision.

"The hell I will!" she screamed back, though it hurt to do so. "Hunter, he's weakened. We took away five of the souls. Fight."

"I said, shut—up."

Bailey braced herself for another backhand, but instead he picked up the material he'd dropped onto the ground and started shoving it at her mouth as she struggled to turn her head away as much as possible.

"Hunter. Help me. Please. I know you can fight him. Fight him!"

He grabbed her by the back of the head and held her in place enough to force the material into her mouth.

"Now where's that duct tape?" He backed away.

Bailey gagged on the material and fought with the muscles in her face and mouth to expel the thing. She had to reach Hunter before he succeeded in silencing her. It was her only chance.

"I'll use yours. You just stay quiet," he said, bending over Charity in the corner.

Bailey began to swing, using her legs to pump herself back and forth as he ripped the tape from Charity's mouth.

"Please, let her go," Charity said, in a weak and frightened voice.

"Be quiet, or I'll cut out your tongue."

Bailey swung forward, thrusting her feet at his bent over backside, and shoved with all her might. He fell onto Charity, and Bailey worked the rest of the stuff from her mouth.

"Hunter!" she shrieked. "Hunter, come back to us."

She started to cry as he less than gracefully worked his way to his feet and crossed over to her.

"Hunter," she wept.

He picked up the scalpel and swung it out toward her in an arc, long arm outstretched. She ducked her head to the side, but the blade missed by a mile as he reached for the rope above her wrists. Hunter held her close with one arm as he stretched up on his toes to cut through her bonds with his other hand. She fell into him as her wrists were finally freed, shoulders filled with pain, and burns on her skin where the rope had pulled against her weight.

"Is it you?" she asked, hardly daring to hope.

"It's me," he said, stroking her bruised face. His eyes beautiful and warm like cocoa, and not red like Satan. "You gave me the strength to fight him, Bailey. You saved me."

Bailey relaxed against him, hiccupping between sobs and huge gulps of air. She let him undo the rest of her bonds and help her to the stairs leading to his room, before going to release Charity. Every movement was pain, but Bailey used what was left of her adrenaline to climb the steps and lift the door. She climbed awkwardly onto the wood floor and lay on her back, staring at the ceiling. The trap door slammed shut, and as she turned to see what was happening, the heavy carpet rolled back in place above it, separating her from Hunter and Charity.

"What?" she said, through a swollen jaw.

"I told you I didn't need a body, Bailey. Weren't you listening?"

His voice was all around her, invading every bit of air in the room, turning it to ice against her tender skin.

"I freed Hunter." She couldn't work her way to a standing position.

"Until he finds your body, breaks down, and I slip inside him again."

Bailey reached for the door as Hunter pounded on the other side of it. She could hear his muffled cries from beneath the carpet.

"Hunter!" she screamed, as hands grabbed her by the hips and began to drag her back along the floor.

Clawing her way back toward the door, Bailey couldn't stop screaming.

"Bailey!" Hunter yelled, through the boards. "What's happening? Let me in."

"He can't get in," Beckham's voice taunted as he yanked her backward again.

Bailey fought to get back to Hunter, breaking her nails on the floor as she tried to drag herself away from the force behind, and now on top of her.

"You're going to die now, Bailey," Beckham breathed over her ear.

Bailey stopped struggling for a moment. Hunter couldn't get in. She had no more help coming. Dottie had used her energy to give her the information earlier. But Bailey could do something important before her death. She had a choice and a way to thwart him, even if she couldn't fight him off physically. With one last burst of strength, she dragged her body forward and called through to Hunter.

"Get Charity and the jars and get them out," Bailey shrieked. "Can you hear me? Get them all out past the tree."

A force that felt like a million hands pulled Bailey up off the ground and slammed her against the wall, almost to the edge of the ceiling, arms and legs splayed outward and held in place with the weight of what felt like an elephant.

"You would try to defy me as your final act?" His voice reverberated throughout the room and inside her chest cavity.

"It's not about you. It's about not leaving anyone behind if I can possibly help them."

She struggled against her invisible bonds as fingers closed around her throat. She could feel a large man's body, *Beckham's body*, stretched over hers in a very personal way, his bushy sideburns rubbing against the tender skin of her cheek. She understood now what Caleb felt in those last minutes. He'd sacrificed his life so Amber would be safe. Amber and Bailey and everyone else who could've been hurt. He was never abandoning her. He was saving her.

"Die, bitch." The voice echoed through the room as fingers pressed in, cutting off her oxygen supply, once again making lights pop in her vision.

Her body jerked as she struggled to find the smallest trickle of air. A buzzing sounded in her head as her limbs grew heavy and tingly. Had Hunter stopped trying to break through? Was he listening to what she'd said, or was she simply no longer able to hear?

"It's over now, Bailey. I'm going to claim your body now, and then your soul."

No! She was filled with hate as fingers pried at the edges of the last bit of clothing on her body.

"You're mine, Bailey. I wanted you to suffer more in your body, but I'll take the rest of eternity making you suffer in death."

She tried to move, to fight, to kick or scream, but darkness crept into the corers of her vision as her body stopped obeying and stilled, like her brain no longer connected to the rest of her. This was it. With any luck, she'd pass out before she felt any more pain.

As though he read her thoughts, the fingers on her throat relaxed, letting her suck in oxygen, along with a horrible wheezing sound. She knew he wanted her to suffer, and she braced herself for his assault. But instead of more torture, Bailey's eyesight returned with a vision of golden light swirling around the dark shadow of a gigantic man in the air, above the middle of the room. On the floor below stood a circle of glowing white figures, hands raised toward the immense shadow figure writhing in the light above.

Deep, guttural screams filled every inch of space in the room as the golden glow grew brighter and more chaotic, swirling and lashing at the shadow in the center of it. Gilded ropes of light slashed through the dense darkness, hacking pieces of him away, where they sizzled into wisps of black smoke that dissipated.

Bailey didn't know if she was hallucinating in the last moments of death, or if this was actually happening. Either way, she didn't think she could stay conscious much longer. Her eyelids grew heavy, and each wheeze struggling to pull air into her lungs was a battle. Still, she couldn't peel her gaze away from the shadow being destroyed in front of her. It was no more than the torso left now, and the screams had grown softer. Or was it her fading?

The door to the bedroom slammed open somewhere nearby, and Sergeant Harper's voice cut through the insanity.

"Holy shit."

Bailey felt the invisible bonds on her body finally release, letting her slide down the wall and into strong arms. Then everything went black.

CHAPTER 27

Bailey woke to the sounds of beeping equipment, a strong antiseptic smell, and an annoying itch on her arm that she couldn't scratch because her limbs were too heavy to lift. She groaned and blinked as the memories all flooded back.

"She's waking up," her father yelled from somewhere to her right,

Bailey winced. "Not so loud," she croaked. Her voice came out as more of a hoarse crackle than actual words.

"Shh." Her father hushed, smoothing back her hair like when she was a baby. "Don't try to talk. Your voice box is bruised."

"Along with the rest of you," Tom said from her left, surprising her.

Bailey forced her eyes open all the way and looked around. She was in a hospital bed surrounded by her father, Estrella, Tom, and Hunter, who hung back in the corner, foot up against the wall, his hands stuffed in his pockets.

"We were so scared, sweetheart." Her father leaned in for another hug.

"Easy there, give her some air, Gerry," Estrella said.

Bailey opened her mouth again and someone shoved a marker in her hand, along with a small whiteboard. She didn't like it, but she'd do it until it became easier to talk.

Where's Charity?

"She's waiting to be cleared to leave her room," her dad said. "I'm looking forward to when you're well enough to explain why you thought you'd go off on your own yet again, looking for a murderer."

"The important thing is that she's okay," Estrella said, voice thick with emotion as she squeezed Bailey's hand.

Okay, was a relative term. Alive, was more accurate.

Where's Harper, she wrote on the whiteboard.

"Sergeant Harper?" Estrella asked. "He's waiting to speak with you."

Bailey noticed her father shoot Estrella a look, so she yanked on his hand.

He sighed. "I didn't think you should be bothered yet about what you've been through."

Bailey rolled her eyes and scribbled on her board.

I want to see him.

"Okay." Her father pried himself away from the bed, Estrella and Tom following him out.

Hunter stood to leave also, but Bailey raised a hand. "Wait," she whispered, the word scraping her raw throat like rusty nails.

Hunter moved quickly to her side and kneeled at the bed. "You really can't stop talking, can you?" he asked with the smile that first melted her heart.

She shook her head.

"Bailey," he said softly, like her name was something fragile. "I'm so sorry."

She shook her head again, reaching up to stroke his face. *It's not your fault,* she tried to say, but he stopped her with a soft kiss on her cracked lips, the touch like the brush of a butterfly's wing, and the ones in her stomach fluttered in response.

"I was so miserable about Fynn, the idiot turning himself in." He pulled back and stroked her hair. "I felt so helpless to do anything about it, and the next thing I knew I was hearing your voice from afar, screaming for my help, and I was trapped somewhere dark and couldn't get to you."

Bailey reached up to put her hand on his as he blinked back tears. "Then I saw everything like a sudden bright light. I saw it all from above, like I was floating over my own body. I saw you screaming for me, tied up like that, and what he'd done to you, and the weapon in my hand with your blood on it." His voice broke with emotion and his hand trembled beneath hers. "And I lunged at him—at me—and I was back in my body, holding that thing."

Bailey wanted to tell him he'd done it, that he'd banished Beckham when no one else could, but she couldn't speak, so she did the next best thing and brought his hand to her mouth to kiss it.

He smiled down at her through his tears. "Thanks for believing in me. For not leaving me trapped in the dark."

Harper cleared his throat from behind, and Hunter dropped his head down onto Bailey, above the sheets.

"Sorry to interrupt, lovebirds, but I hear you're eager to make a statement, Miss Thompson." Harper strode over to the bed and took a seat at Bailey's side, opposite Hunter.

"I'm not leaving." Hunter raised his head, holding her hand.

"No need." Harper took out a small notebook and pen. "Before we begin, I understand you're to use a whiteboard for communication, Miss Thompson. Doctor's orders. Anyway, being that this is such an unusual case, I thought perhaps I would start with what I saw. I'm hoping you can fill in some of the missing details and help explain what actually happened."

Bailey nodded, withdrawing her hand from Hunter's to use her marker once again.

Harper knows everything, she wrote, and showed them both.

Hunter's head snapped around to gawk at the Sergeant.

"Your girlfriend here stopped by the office while you were visiting your brother."

"Not me," Hunter said softly, and Bailey's heart squeezed.

"She told me quite a story. And believe me, I've heard a few over the years. The thing is, everything she said—all the facts—checked out and corroborate her story, including the identity of the two bodies found in the attic. Which left me with a predicament, as you can imagine."

You came to the house, Bailey wrote.

"Yes, ma'am. I came to check out the story you told me about the secret passage, and since you said it ended up in Mr. Callahan's room, I figured that was the best place to start, since finding anything by that tree seemed unlikely any time this century."

"Thank God you got there in time," Hunter said.

Harper sighed and re-crossed his legs. "What I saw when I opened that door was impossible. What I saw was Miss Thompson being held over eight feet up in the air, against the wall. She was clearly under attack. And forgive me for being indelicate, but had most of her clothing removed and had suffered obvious injuries."

Bailey's throat felt tight again and she gingerly probed the outside of it, unable to meet either man's eyes.

"But in the room itself, I saw…" He cleared his throat and took a deep breath. "Well, the best I can describe it, there were people, glowing people, and something swirling in the middle, a flash of light, and then they were gone. At that time, I saw Miss Thompson here slide down the wall like something had dropped her. Luckily, my reflexes are still good enough that I was able to catch her and prevent any more damage or broken bones."

Thank you, Bailey wrote.

"You're very welcome. I wish I'd been there sooner, Miss Thompson. Though, I wish you wouldn't keep taking matters into your own hands."

Bailey nodded.

"So, here's the thing." He uncrossed his legs and leaned forward, conspiratorially. "What the hell did I see, if this ghost or ghoul or whatever he was, used real bodies to do his dirty work?"

"Bailey had just gotten him out of my body," Hunter said. "I'm guessing Charity didn't tell you because she didn't want me to get in trouble like Fynn. But he was using me, and I can tell you firsthand that I wasn't aware of a single thing until Bailey started calling to me."

Harper's eyes opened wide beneath his spectacles. "I see. So, when you were free, he decided to go ahead and attack Miss Thompson, without a body, so to speak."

Bailey held up the whiteboard with the sentence she'd been frantically writing since Harper's question.

He told me he didn't need a body. He used them because he liked to mess with his victims' heads and frame the living.

Harper stroked his chin for a minute. "So, the question becomes, how do we prove a freaking ghost is responsible?"

"You believe us?" Hunter asked.

"I saw it with my own eyes, and I always believe my own eyes."

Bailey scribbled again and they both waited as she worked, but her question was solely for Hunter.

You listened to what I asked when I screamed through the door?

Hunter smiled and squeezed her hand. "I did what you said right away. I took Charity and the remains back out past the tree."

Bailey had freed them as her last desperate act, refusing to leave anyone behind. And they came back for her as well.

She fought back her tears as she silently thanked Dottie and the others. She scribbled at the board in her hand.

What you saw, Sergeant, were his victims coming back to serve justice on their own.

"I've removed all the remaining body parts as evidence," Harper said, answering her unasked question about Beckham's mother and sister. "But it sounds like he won't be torturing any souls from here on out."

Bailey nodded.

"What do we do about Fynn?" Hunter asked.

Harper grunted and sat back in the chair.

"That's a bit trickier. Miss Tucker regained consciousness and identified him as her attacker."

Bailey held on tight to Hunter's hand as he sat back hard on his heels.

"However, I had a little chat with her, and with the help of your friend, Miss Morgan, we were able to explain what happened, as best we could, to her family and attorney. They've agreed not to press charges, under several conditions."

Exhaustion threatened to pull Bailey's head back onto the comfort of the pillow, but she fought it, blinking.

"What?" she croaked, too tired to use the whiteboard anymore.

"Her lawyers asked for a restraining order against the entire Callahan family."

A laugh burst from Hunter. "I think we can handle that."

"And they want the rights to the story, so to speak. Apparently, they're convinced that she can find some sort of fame and fortune as the living victim of a real-life ghost attack. They've been in contact with several movie studios, as I understand it."

"I don't know how Mama will cope with all that attention around us and the house."

"I don't think they'll use the real house." Harper said. "So, you have nothing to worry about. She can't if you're there. Restraining order and all."

Hunter nodded, settling down next to Bailey, seemingly relieved.

"You need rest, Miss Thompson." Harper leaned in to pat her hand, awkwardly. "You've been through a lot, and you've certainly opened my eyes. No matter the unconventionality of it, no innocent men will be going to prison on my watch. I promise you that."

Gratitude swelled in Bailey's heart and she threw her heavy arms around Harper's neck. His rough cheek pressed against hers. He smelled like coffee grounds, comforting and warm.

"Thank you, Miss Thompson." He carefully set her back on the bed and patted her head. "You want to go get something to eat, Mr. Callahan? You've been here for nearly twenty-four hours. I think she's going to sleep awhile, and I for one could use a coffee."

"No, thanks," Hunter said. "I'm not leaving her side again."

Harper nodded and left the room, shutting the door behind him on his way out.

Bailey patted the spot next to her on the bed and Hunter crawled in beside her, careful not to knock any of the tubes or machines surrounding her. He maneuvered his arm around her and she snuggled into his side, inhaling his scent of cinnamon and fresh-baked goodness, wondering if he'd be open to letting her borrow one of his shirts to sleep in.

"You are the bravest person I know." He cocked his head so that his intense cocoa eyes were focused only on her.

Bailey's neck warmed as she smiled up at him. "Thanks," she whispered. "I think it runs in the family."

Hunter nodded and reached his free hand up to caress her cheek, letting his thumb pass back and forth over her skin, which suddenly felt like it had a million tiny electric charges going off beneath his touch.

"You're also the smartest and most beautiful person I know." Hunter's voice was deep and soft, his eyes hypnotic.

"Ditto," Bailey whispered, ready to drown in a sea of cocoa.

"So..." Hunter brought his face so close she could feel his breath mingle with hers. "Now that you've solved the mystery of the Gallows House, will you still want to visit?"

Bailey grinned. "I'd be interested in visiting, as long as you're there."

Hunter closed the distance between them, and Bailey sunk into the blissful sensation of their kiss.

The best part about giving her heart to Hunter was knowing she could trust him with it and that whatever they may go through from here on out, they'd do it together.

ABOUT THE AUTHOR

Lisa lives with her husband the rocket scientist and their three junior mad scientists in Southern California. She writes books so she can have an excuse to live in the fantasy world in her head. She likes to share these with readers. She has a parrot and two adopted bunnies who, she is convinced, plan to take over the world with their cuteness. She would most definitely adopt a werewolf as well if she weren't allergic. She loves to chat so don't be shy, send a message or find her on social media.

Connect with Lisa:
Website – lisagailgreen@gmail.com
Instagram – @authorlisagailgreen
Facebook – facebook.com/lisagail.green
Twitter – @lisagailgreen
Pinterest – pinterest.com/lisagailgreen

www.BOROUGHSPUBLISHINGGROUP.com

If you enjoyed this book, please write a review. Our authors appreciate the feedback, and it helps future readers find books they love. We welcome your comments and invite you to send them to info@boroughspublishinggroup.com. Follow us on Facebook, Twitter and Instagram, and be sure to sign up for our newsletter for surprises and new releases from your favorite authors.

Are you an aspiring writer? Check out www.boroughspublishinggroup.com/submit and see if we can help you make your dreams come true.